THE SEVEN ACTS

This book was designed and produced by Silver Goat Media, LLC. Fargo, ND U.S.A. www.silvergoatmedia.com SGM and the SGM goat are trademarks of Silver Goat Media, LLC.

Cover art: "Savage Seven – with Glock and Chocolate."
© 2019 SGM

Cover design: Jonathan Rutter and Peter Schultz
© 2019 SGM

This book was typeset by Cady Ann Rutter.

ISBN-10: 1-944296-14-X
ISBN-13: (Silver Goat Media) 978-1-944296-14-8

A portion of the annual proceeds from the sale of this book is donated to the Longspur Prairie Fund.
www.longspurprairie.org

Started by **KICK**STARTER

First SGM printing – July 2019, Fargo, ND. 1.0 – 010719
Printed and bound in the United States of America.

Malcolm Strand

SGM

This book is for Mrs. Hoime.

I

1

Hello.

To anybody reading this, my name is Michael Beatrice Evans.

And I'm dead.

I'm sitting next to five pounds of gunpowder, a grenade launcher, three guns, and a bottle of Molotov. I'm hiding in a bunker under my parents' basement. The cops are lookin' for me. They're right above me; I can hear 'em up there walkin' around.

I fucked up, see?

My piss and shit are in a bucket sitting inches from my nose. I'm eating out-of-date Ramen noodles like a homeless college boy. The rusty stovetop I've got here has caught fire three times . . . and screw this—I'm sick of hiding!

2

Okay.
I'm calm.
No point exploding.
Especially to you.
I'm fucked.
I fucked myself.
It's my fault.
Sorry.
That's it.
Goodbye.

3

I'm bad at first impressions.

Caught on to that in the sixth grade.

Maybe you *are* wondering how I got stuck next to a keg of gunpowder and a bucket of poo.

Maybe you *do* wanna hear my story.

I'll tell you, but be warned: The events leading up to the present are so fuckin' asinine, they'd be worthy of the Golden Raspberry Award—and that doesn't count the truly horrific shit that just went down a few days ago.

Anyway, this tale's gotta start somewhere.

The day of my birth is as good a place as any.

4

I was born July 16, 1999. I weighed nine pounds. I was fourteen inches long. When I left the hospital, my mother had a scar on her stomach from the C-section. My older brother greeted me at home with a stupid smile; he wouldn't stop shaking my crib, even when it looked like my brains were leaking out of my ears. He was crazy strong, even as a toddler. Then there was the big scare when I got tuberculosis at day thirty. I almost died. Tuberculosis is no joke. Anyway, I proceeded to cough the last dust from my lungs and "miraculously" survived. After that, I received a double ear infection for my first Christmas—Thanks, Santa!—and almost got eaten alive by fungal spores for my first Easter— Thanks, Jesus! I was sick on-again, off-again until

I was about two and a half. These illnesses and "miraculous" recoveries became problems later; I'll talk about that in a bit.

By the time I was four, my parents had decided I was smart. They found me writing "Philadelphia" and some other long words on my mom's whiteboard one morning. Both my parents had graduated college by then—they're no dummies either. They had both my brother and me early, right out of school. My brother's name is Thomas Beatrice Evans, by the way. He's seventeen, a year older than me. He was my right-hand man, up to this point. But he's not here now.

5

My first day at kindergarten was stupid, to say the least, but I remember it. We were putting our things into our cubbies. The teacher decided to be a dick, singled me out 'cause I put my backpack in different.

"Keep your pockets *up* so you can get at them more *easily*, Michael," she said.

I shrugged. "Does it matter?"

She gave me a look. "Are we being *naughty* today, Michael? Do we need to be sent to the principal's office?"

I wanted to punch her. Badly.

But I decided to explain myself. "My stuff isn't in my front pockets. They're in this little pouch here." I showed her.

She scoffed, knelt to my level, and said, "Well, you *still* aren't following the *rules*, Michael. I'm going to have to call someone to take you down to the office *right* now."

She sniffed, got up, and walked away.

"But why the fuck does it matter?" I shouted at her back. "I gave you a straight answer! Why can't you give me one, shitbird?"

I spent the whole day in the office.

Totally worth it.

At least I thought so then.

6

From that day on, I bad-mouthed every teacher who talked down to me.

Kindergarten, elementary school, middle school— all the way up.

Oh, and my parents knew it.

Every night, my mother, a devout Catholic and a lay ecclesial minister, forced me to read young Christian books hoping that I'd learn about the greatness of God. Despite her best attempts to get me to love the Lord, I grew to hate him. I guess the idea of basing my existence on the worship of a person who made the universe in seven days and then pissed off, never to return, annoyed me a little. However, I did start to realize that not every teacher was out to fuck me over.

Then high school rolled around. Tenth grade. I promised myself I wouldn't let anything phase me. I made it through first semester with flying colors and straight A's.

For the first time in my life, I gave a shit.

Then the second semester began.

It was the start of the events that led me here.

7

Super Bowl XLIX was on. The New England Patriots and the Seattle Seahawks duking it out in the most over-hyped football game of the year. I'd always been something of a gambler, and I wanted to test out my recent victories on something riskier.

So I decided to bet on the Seahawks.

I'd looked over the two teams; the Seahawks were primed for a win.

In retrospect, I should've been wary that every experienced gambler at school was betting on the Patriots. Money doesn't make a man logical.

The night of the game, I cheered for my team until my throat burned. But they blew it, those sons of bitches. Lost to a pack of sore winners accused of Deflategate.

I came to school the next day $20,000 in the hole.

Maybe for you $20,000 isn't much.

For a 16 year old?

It's a lot.

Most everyone expected me to pay up in sixty days. A few were willing to give me 'til the end of the semester. I ransacked my wallet, spare change, and even the bank account my parents set up for me.

$306.72 total.

So I sold everything I had. My Xbox 360? Sold. My bike? Sold. My grandmother's rubies? Turned out to be made up of more plastic than Paris Hilton's face.

$746.36 total.

I couldn't get a decent job at my age. And even if I could, it'd take me at least a year to make over nineteen grand.

Couldn't tell my parents either. They'd kill me. Especially my mom.

I needed to come up with over nineteen grand in two months.

It was a problem neither a job nor my parents could solve.

On top of that, I still had to be nice to my teachers, do my chores, keep the grades up, and try to keep my mom chill.

So yeah.

Like I said.

Fucked.

8

I spent the rest of the week moping around, scheming how to get the money. No way was I gonna tell my parents—or any of my relatives—about my debts. Not even my Uncle Edward. He'd struck it rich investing in unicorn tech companies in Silicon Valley. He's so loaded that he engraves his Christmas cards onto gold-leaf plates and spends all his time throwing hundreds at strippers in Las Vegas.

Eddie's twenty-three years old.

So yeah. I thought about asking him for some cash, but he tends to run his mouth at family reunions, and he hates my dad's guts, so no help there. One word to the old man about this and I'd be doubly fucked, so Uncle Eddie was out. I considered odd jobs, but there's no way I could rake in enough dough. Nothing I thought of could make the cash I needed. Night after night, I'd march down to my basement room, spin up a plan, realize it was garbage, then go to bed feeling like shit.

9

The only people who noticed my state of mind were my friends. Haven't mentioned them yet. They're the only other ones besides my brother and my parents who give a shit about me.

There's Ryan, my best friend since first grade. He gets pessimistic and doesn't hesitate to criticize, but he's like a second brother because of our shared cynicism. We'd slowly drifted apart the past few months, and his negative-Nancy attitude only got worse as tenth grade marched on.

There's Logan, the comedian of our group, a joy to be around. Coolest kid I know. His lighthearted attitude on just about everything cheers us up all the time; just a goofy, outgoing black kid. Love the guy.

And then there's Catherine. Kat, for short. She's nice and skilled at all things computers. Super smart.

So that's everyone.

I'm serious.

It's hard finding friends when your whole school thinks you're a deranged delinquent who cusses out all the teachers.

It's especially hard when it's true.

10

So a week after the Super Bowl.

Everyone was still talking about the stupid-ass play the Seahawks made. But besides that, it was business as usual. My creditors continued to follow me in the hallways, looking for their money. One of them—can't remember who—decided to trip me. Pure class, that prick. I flailed in the air, books flying, and fell on my face.

Assholes.

But then a hand stuck out. "You all right, dude?"

I looked up.

It was Kat. I took her hand and stood up. "Yeah, I'm fine. Tired of being harassed by these jack-offs. Most of 'em said two months."

Logan and Ryan strolled up.

"Ooh, did I almost catch somethin' happenin' over here?" Logan grinned.

I punched him lightly. "You just wanna see some PDA 'cause you don't get any action yourself."

Logan pretended to be hurt.

"Yeah," I said. "That's right. Get fucked."

He fired back. "Yeah, right. The only person 'round here who's been fucked recently is your mom. And lemme tell you, buddy, she found me *very* handsome, very black, and very *big* . . . ."

"Christ, Logan!" Kat tried not to laugh, picking up some of my books. "What is this, middle school?"

"Moving on," Ryan interjected, shaking his head.

"You got anything going on this weekend, Michael? We were thinking about hitting the DQ and then rolling to Logan's. His mom is hanging with her cousin over in Pocatello this week."

I picked up the last of my books. "Yeah, about that." I sighed. "Got a lot of thinking to do. Don't have a clue what to do about my debt. Fuckin' Seahawks."

Ryan rolled his eyes. "Jesus, Michael. What's the point of figuring all this out alone when you've got us to help?"

"Come on, Mikey," Kat said. "Come with." She took out several slips of paper and handed one to me.

It was a coupon for a free Dilly Bar.

She winked. "You won't even have to pay."

"I'll think about it," I said.

Logan wrapped his arm around me as everyone else walked off. "You sure you can't make it Friday? We'll help you figure it out, bro. It'll be fun."

I shrugged. "Dunno yet. Tell you tomorrow if I can think of something."

"Gotcha. See you around."

11

After school, I left cross-country practice, got home, and found dinner made. I quickly put together a plate of my mom's garbage food. She can't cook for shit—except her spaghetti, that shit's fuckin' delicious. I sat down to join my family at the table, expecting an onslaught of questions as soon as I started eating.

"So." My brother Thomas winked. "How's your day?"

There it was.

"Fine," I said as I dug in.

"May the Lord save us from your 'fine.'" Mom preached. "You and God both know more things happened today than 'fine' things. I wish you would tell the truth, Michael."

"Yeah, Mike," Dad said. "Let's use my day as an example: Today, my street officers ended up apprehending ten speeders. One going fifteen over, and another over twenty-five."

My dad is a police officer for Normal, Idaho. That's the town where I live. Probably should have mentioned that earlier. Anyway, it's boring. We grow potatoes. I wish there was more to say about it. Maybe I could say half the men are religious assholes who knock on doors to preach "God's way," despite hating Mormons for doing the same thing, and the other half contribute to our proud achievement of the highest crime rate in Idaho. It's embarrassing. For a town that grows starchy vegetables, there's a lot of seedy stuff going on.

"Earth to Michael?" Mom asked. "Hello?"

I looked up. Mom was looking at me in that way. "Tell us about your day, please."

I threw my hands in the air. "How else am I supposed to explain an average day with nothing good, bad, or noteworthy in it besides the word 'fine'? Do you want me to break into song and dance while I'm at it?"

"Smartass," Thomas snorted.

I sighed. "Look, can I please be excused? I'm tired."

I didn't bother to hear the answer. I stood up, tramped downstairs to my room, and thought about my dilemma until I fell asleep at my desk chair.

12

The next day was Thursday. I talked to my friends at the end of school and declined their offer to help. They hung their heads.

"Fine, Michael," Ryan sighed. "I guess I should've known you'd say 'no.' But we're here for you, man. Don't forget."

I nodded. Ryan smirked. "See you around, bud."

My friends walked away. I stood in the middle of the hallway, feeling sorry for myself, thinking hard about the debt. All my ideas sucked.

I was still fucked.

Then someone slammed me to the ground, muscly hands at my neck, choking me.

"Get . . . off . . . me . . .!" I tried to scream, tried to breathe.

A man growled in response. "Where's my money, Evans? Where's my six hundred goddamn bucks?"

"You said . . . I could pay you . . . in two months."

"I need it *now*. So where is it, big gamblin' man? Huh? Gonna have to squeeze the life out of you to get it?!"

"Think I'm gonna have it after a week, dumbass?" I squeaked. "You want your money so bad? Fine. Here's your six hundred bucks." I tried a manly kick at my assailant. That shit always works in the movies.

His grip tightened.

I was getting dizzy.

"Think you can play with me, boy? That it? Let's see how hard you squeal when you're knocked the fuck out!"

Stars spun in my eyes.

SMACK!

My attacker was knocked sideways, dropping like an empty potato sack.

I looked up, gasping.

A big, beefy-ass boy stood over me.

Jim Ulrin, quarterback of the Normal High School football team.

Jim knows me, and I know him. He's one of Ryan's buds, so he hangs with us sometimes. A crazy arrogant guy. He'd be hanging with all the cool kids if he wasn't so ugly. Seriously, this guy's face is a disfigured, Hephaestus-looking abomination, yet he also thinks, at the exact same time, that he's a total stud. The first time I met Jim, he offered to give me front-row tickets to the school stadium to watch him dominate at the homecoming game. I replied by saying he was lucky his head is always under a helmet, otherwise he'd be mistaken for the Elephant Man's bastard child. The nickname "Bastard" stuck. I never called him anything else, despite the ever-present threat of an ass-kicking. But he can be fun to hang around, too. Sometimes.

I stood up, cleared my throat. "Thanks, Bastard. Owe you."

He smirked. "Don't thank me, bro. Thank my bulging biceps." He flexed. "Been working out. Ladies have noticed."

I picked up my stuff and walked to my locker. Bastard followed.

"Doin' anything this weekend?" I asked.

Bastard shrugged. "Hitting the DQ with the gang, crashing at Logan's place. His mom is out of town."

"They invited you?"

"'Course they did!" Bastard laughed. "No hangout would be complete without the superstar! Heard you weren't going. Why's that? Don't like Dairy Queen now?"

"Gotta figure out how I'm gonna pay off my bookies. I owe twenty grand." I sighed. "It's almost like the only option I have left is . . . ." I trailed off.

"Michael?"

A lighting-in-a-bottle idea blasted through my head.

"I'll see you—see you later." I stammered. "I gotta get home."

"What about cross-country practice?" Bastard hollered at my back.

"Skipping. I'll run to my house anyways. Gotta go."

I hauled ass home.

13

In my room, later that afternoon.

Knock, knock, knock on the door.

"I'm busy," I said.

The door opened regardless. Mom stormed into my room, furious.

"Jesus!" I shouted, startled. I scrambled to cover

up the plans and drawings on my desk. "Didn't you hear me?!"

"*Michael Beatrice Evans!*" she yelled. She was a king cobra ready to strike. "Don't you *dare* take the Lord's name in vain!"

The temperature seemed to drop twenty degrees. When I said she was a devout Catholic, I meant it. I dropped my head, muttering an apology.

She decided to give me reprieve. "Why weren't you upstairs for confession? And don't tell me you've nothing to confess; I know you do. God sees the good and the bad in all of us. The good *and* the bad, Michael."

"Look, I'm just doing some math homework," I said. "Is that good? Or bad? Just chill, okay? Nothing to have an aneurysm over."

"Our Lord Jesus died to atone our sins. The least you could do is acknowledge that, Michael. You're a child of God."

"All right, all right. I'll confess. Let me finish my homework, first?"

She thought about this for a few seconds, then sighed. "Be in the confessional in an hour. No later."

She walked upstairs. I made sure the door was shut and locked before going back to work on my plans.

"Crazy lady," I muttered under my breath.

What plans? You might be wondering.

Just wait. I'm getting to that part.

14

"Hey, guys," I said, sitting down with the crew at the lunch table before school. "Figured it out."

Ryan slurped from his juice box. "Figured what out?" he asked. "Your life?"

"Hilarious," I said. Then I looked him in the eye. "Figured out how I'm going to pay my debt."

"Hey, that's great." Kat smiled. "So you'll be coming out with us after school?"

"That's right."

"All right!" Logan cheered, happy guy that he is. "The gang's all here!"

"What you gonna do?" Bastard snorted. "Rob a bank or something?"

The five-minute bell rang.

"Who do you think I am, Bastard?" I laughed, standing up. "It's gonna be way easier than that—and only slightly illegal. Tell you about it after school."

15

Soon enough, we were sitting in the Dairy Queen eating Dilly Bars. I kept quiet while the others discussed the past week, running my plan over in my head, thinking it through from every angle.

It seemed to check out.

The last hurdle to jump was figuring out how I was going to—.

"Michael!" Logan waved a hand in my face. He was wearing his favorite white hoodie. I love it 'cause it makes his face seem even darker. Like a crazy, fun-loving black ghost.

I snapped out of it. "What?"

"I asked if you were gonna show us your plan."

I shook my head. "Not here. Let's do it at your house." I picked up my dessert. "For now, I'd like to enjoy this delicious and nutritious *Dilly Bar*."

Ryan snickered. "Yeah, the Dilly Bar you haven't been eating."

The DQ entrance swung open behind me.

Bastard grinned. "'Sup, Thomas!"

My brother walked to our booth. "How we doing?"

"Fucking fantastic," Logan responded, standing up to shake his hand. "How could we not be? It's *Friday*, bro!"

"Couldn't have said it better myself," I agreed. "What are you doing here, Thomas?"

"Just stopping by, checking in. Hey, you forget to confess this morning?"

I clenched my teeth. "God damn."

"You can say that again. Mom's pretty upset. Unless you wanna be confessing and praying 24/7, you better stop forgetting."

"Why do we need to do this shit, anyways?" I asked. "It's like we're living in the Dark Ages."

"Don't know," Thomas said. "But it's her house, so it's her rules. And you're a 'child of God,' my son. Isn't there something more interesting we could talk about?"

I grinned. "You're right."

My grin got bigger.

"Want a delicious and nutritious Dilly Bar?"

16

We left the Dairy Queen, totally hopped-up on sugar, and cruised over to Logan's, where we went downstairs to his basement. There were some tables and stuff down there, a couple of big couches, and a huge TV that we always used for watching old movies when we'd spend the night.

The perfect place for a secret plan.

We clattered down the steps.

Ryan closed the basement door.

"So." I rubbed my hands together. "Who wants to make some money?"

17

Everyone stared at me, confused.

"What the hell?" Ryan asked. "I mean, I'm always up for making the green, but I thought the point of all this was paying your debt."

"I *will* pay. You'll take the leftovers."

"Ah, I get it, Michael," Logan grinned. "You gonna give us some cash 'cause you such a kind soul? Awfully white of you, bro."

I snorted. "Nice try, buddy. You're gonna work your asses off for it. But seriously—straight up—I need you guys for this to work."

"So what *is* this plan, then?" Thomas asked.

I reached into my jacket pocket and pulled out a slip of paper. "Take a look at this."

Bastard leaned forward. "It's one of those coupons for free Dilly Bars."

Kat looked confused. "What's this gotta do with anything?"

"Where'd I get it?" I asked.

She paused. Then, "Well, I must've. . . ." Her voice faltered. "No. I never gave you a coupon. I used all the coupons I had to pay for ice cream we just ate. So where'd you get it? From the newspaper? What's the big deal?"

"We don't get the newspaper, remember? My mom thinks the owner's a Lutheran heretic. But I did get it from a printer. *My* printer."

It took another second for it to dawn on her.

Everyone's eyes widened.

"You *copied* it?" Ryan laughed.

I waved the forged coupon like a dollar bill. "Minted yesterday, baby. Whatever smart marketing douche-nozzle came up with this didn't think to put a barcode or deadline on it." I dug more wads of paper out of my coat pockets. All of them were the same coupon. I passed them out, like I was dealing cards. "Thirty free Dilly Bars right there, people."

They had different reactions. Logan was curious. Kat frowned. Thomas was amused. Ryan was . . . well, Ryan didn't express emotion that often. I guess he was just okay about it.

Bastard, though . . . .

He tried not to show it, but I knew he was freaking the fuck out. "You're telling me you want us to *steal* Dilly Bars, sell 'em like cocaine on the black market? Fuckin' Dilly dealers? The fuck is wrong with you?"

"'Dilly dealers!'" I laughed. "How many times you heard about kids being arrested for stealing *ice cream*, Bastard?"

He didn't say anything.

I pressed on. "Unless you find some magic money tree or find a doctor's office or law firm looking to hire a tenth grader, this is what I've gotta do. It's gonna work. I can do it."

Bastard stood up. "Yeah. You're right. This is what *you* can do. I'm out."

He took off, up the stairs, and gone.

I sighed. "Ryan, he gonna snitch?"

He shook his head. "He'll come back. I'll talk to him."

I guess I believed him.

And this was no time to stop, so I kept going. "I know what you're thinking—this sounds absolutely moronic. And you know what? You're probably right. But you know what else? It's the only way I could think to get the money I need with the time I've got. We'll take the coupons, buy all the Dilly Bars, start our own ice cream business. It'll be cheaper and easier. We don't have any overhead. We don't even have to make ice cream. When we run out of coupons, we go back, print some more, sell, repeat. Bingo."

Logan shook his head. "You sure it'll work? Like, *actually* work? Or is this just some fantasy that, like, only works in your head?"

I nodded and dragged the whiteboard sitting by the wall over to us. "Where's a dry erase marker?"

Thomas handed me one. I drew a crude map with three highlighted buildings. "These are the three Dairy Queens in Normal, this third one here . . ." I tapped the white board. ". . . on the outskirts of the town, is opening in a few days. With two of us going to each Dairy Queen after school for an hour at a time, we could get a lot of Dilly Bars. I've done the math. The coupon says, 'limit two per customer per day.' If we create several disguises, we could maximize collection and get an average of five to seven bars per person per hour, depending on the number of costumes we make."

"Costumes?" Kat snorted.

"All right." Ryan sighed and leaned back. "We can get the bars. But how are you going to sell 'em?"

"And, how much money is in it for us?" Logan added.

I smiled and kept scrawling on the whiteboard. "I've picked three points farthest away from the Dairy Queens. We can sell the treats like street vendors. They're on busy streets, so we can catch commuters and kids and stuff on their way to work or school or wherever. As for the second question, about the cash: It's a nice amount. Since Dilly Bars cost $1.59, and if we sell, with Bastard involved, about thirty-six per hour, four hours a day, for forty-five days—keeping in mind any little hiccups we might run into—we'd earn a little over ten grand. Keep in mind, only about half of my creditors need the money in the first sixty days, so that leaves us a little more time to pay back the rest by semester's end. Maximizing the days we have available, we'd have an additional seventy-five days to collect the money, which leaves us with about seven thousand in surplus. Taking out $500 for materials, coolers, ink, and shit like that—and putting back my earnings, of course— and with Bastard in the picture, you'll each net about $1,300."

"*Costumes*?" Kat repeated.

I capped the marker. "I spent last night working on this. The math checks out. Just can't do it on my own. And, yes. *Costumes*. It's not hard. Ever watch James Bond?"

Silence for a few seconds.

My friends looked at each other.

Then Logan put his hand in first and winked at me. "It might not work, but what the hell?"

"I like costumes." Kat put her hand in. "With you to the end." She smiled. This isn't a love story. That's a promise. But when Kat smiles at you, it stops your heart.

Ryan shoved both hands in and shouted: "That's some easy-ass Dilly money right there!"

Everyone laughed.

But Thomas hesitated. He was normally a little wary of my schemes, and the fact that it was totally illegal didn't help. He was his father's son, after all. But he finally put his hand in. "Let's do this."

"Sweet." I said. "Wanna watch *Alien*?"

"Hell yeah!" Logan exclaimed. "You guys sit down—I'll get the popcorn."

"I can only stay for one!" Kat yelled. "Make mine extra-buttery!"

It was settled.

They were in it to the end.

For better or worse.

Turns out—it was worse.

Way worse.

18

About sixteen hours earlier, Michael crept to the printer in his living room. He'd stayed up working on his plans while his parents slept. Quietly, he took out a slip of paper and set it on the printer's glass.

He closed the flap.

Pressed COPY.

The printer churned and hummed.

The copies came out, fresh and warm.

Picking up a scissors, he cut out the copy so it looked exactly like the original.

Then he crumpled up the scraps and threw them in the garbage bin.

He was ready to begin.

All he needed were his friends.

19

That night, staying over at Logan's, I had one of the worst nightmares of my life.

It wasn't as bad as what actually happened that night, but I'm telling you now because it matters for what comes later, all right?

I was in a grand chapel, standing in line at the confessional. It was totally silent save for the quiet whispers of the confessors. Each one entered the confessional and then came out—with blood on their faces.

"Next," a bishop hissed from the dark.

I walked into the confessional and sat on the bench.

It was uncomfortably hot.

There was no lattice wall; it was completely enclosed.

A woman's voice whispered in my head, "You must confess, Michael, for you have sinned. Confess, child of God."

The air grew hotter. And hotter.

I thought my eyebrows were burning off.

The voice whispered again, "You must confess, Michael, for you have sinned."

There was a loud "POP!"—almost like a small bomb—and the confessional burst into flames.

A mob of priests and nuns surrounded me.

They weren't whispering now.

They were shouting my name.

"Michael! You must confess! Michael! You have sinned! Michael! Child of God!"

I bolted awake, smoke in my eyes, orange light everywhere.

"I confess!" I screamed.

"Michael!" Logan screamed again. "We gotta go! The fuckin' *house* is on fire!"

And it was.

Smoke everywhere, the sound of roaring flames. Logan grabbed me, pulled me off the couch. The air was so thick that it felt like I was breathing hot cotton. I gasped, staying low and coughing my way upstairs toward the back door. I stepped outside into the cold air, the snow wet beneath my socks. Logan kept pushing me, pushing me away from the house, the orange glow and heat at my back.

I turned around to see the destruction.

Logan's house was burning. There was a huge

hole in the roof of the house. Support beams were collapsing one by one, almost in slow motion—and then the central section gave way. The entire house went down in a roar of flames.

Thomas walked up to me. "Not how I wanted to wake up. You leave the popcorn kettle on or something?"

Logan shook his head, ignoring Thomas's joke. He was in shock. Somehow, his dark face managed to seem pale.

"See, this is why this world sucks," Ryan said.

"Ryan, chill," Kat said quietly. "We don't know what happened."

"We know *exactly* what happened!" Ryan shouted.

"What's the mystery? Logan's fuckin' house *burned down!*"

I looked back at Logan. He was really stunned. I walked closer to him. For some reason, I couldn't stop thinking about my dream. "You okay?"

He watched the blaze. "I guess I'm fine," he answered. His eyes were glassy. The firemen arrived, started hosing the flames. "But my mom is gonna freak."

20

About two hours later, after a thorough soaking, all traces of flame were gone. Smoke rose feebly from the soggy heap. A fireman walked over and started talking to Logan's mom. She'd come back from Pocatello when a neighbor had called. We sat on the hood of Logan's mom's car.

Then my mom drove up in our minivan.

"Oh, man." Thomas elbowed me in the side.

"We gotta go, Logan." I patted him on the shoulder, then glanced at Thomas. He was still looking at Mom in the minivan.

Logan nodded. "Michael, I can still help with the plan, starting Monday. Don't you worry about me."

I gave him a hug.

Do you see how he was? Dude's house was a pile of ashes, but for some reason, he was still worried about *me*.

"Thanks, man," I said. "Really appreciate it." Then I looked at Ryan. "You gonna be able to convince Bastard to join us?"

He shrugged. "I think so."

"Good. All right"

Thomas and I headed toward the minivan.

"You think we're gonna get chewed out?" I asked.

My brother nodded. "I know *you* definitely will."

"Why?" I asked.

We got in the van, and Mom turned around to face me. Her voice was calm as she lifted her chin at Logan's house. "This is what happens when you miss confession."

Can you believe that shit?

21

When we got home, Mom shooed Thomas downstairs to his room, then she sat me down at the dining room table.

"What did I tell you Thursday?" she asked.

I tried to give her my best, most defiant stare. "You told me to have a good day at school."

"Don't sass me," she said. "Thou shalt honor thy father and mother."

I knew what she wanted. So I said it. "You told me to go to confession every day."

"And what *didn't* you do yesterday?"

"I don't think I took out the trash."

"Michael." She closed her eyes. "This is serious."

"I didn't go to confession."

She held up her finger. "I'm giving you one more chance to face your sins. If you aren't in confession tomorrow morning, then we'll take the next steps."

I didn't want to know what the next steps were, so I decided the best thing to do would be to nod.

"Good. No leaving the house this weekend, you understand?"

She got up and walked away.

"Bitch," I muttered to myself, but it was half-hearted.

I went downstairs, peeked my head into Thomas's room. He was listening to music.

"Got a second?" I asked.

He nodded.

I opened his door. "Come on."

He followed me into my room. I walked over to the corner near my bed, ripped up the loose corner of carpet.

Beneath the carpet, there was an iron manhole cover stamped with these words: NORMAL CITY SEWER.

"What the hell?"

I grinned. "The show must go on."

22

We climbed down the ladder into the sewer. I gagged the moment I stepped onto the cement floor.

"Good God," Thomas choked. "The smell!"

He backed away from the ladder, almost puked. "Holy shit," he sputtered.

"This place is rancid," I agreed and laughed, doing my best to hold onto my cookies. "But, yeah—wish we brought something to mask the stench."

"Just give it time." He plugged his nose. "I'm bringing clothespins tomorrow." Then he laughed. "Why's there a sewer under your bedroom?"

I grinned. "You know how Normal burned to the ground in the 60s? Before then, the sewer they used was called a combined sewer. It carried both stormwater and sewage together and separated them near the drainage pipe using gravity. When Normal burned down, they rebuilt the two systems separately, leaving the old system to slowly dry out over time."

"Perfect hiding place." He nodded, still holding his nose. "If you don't mind the smell. Why'd you never tell me about this?"

"Man's gotta have his secrets."

23

We went down and started walking, using my phone's flashlight to see.

"Michael?" Thomas interrupted. "Where are we

going? We've taken three rights since we started moving."

I took the sewer blueprints out of my pocket that I'd printed the previous morning.

"Let's see." I put a finger where we were. "We've got three more lefts, a right, and a left, and the destination should be to our right."

"All right. But what *is* the destination?"

"To get the costumes."

"Where?"

"JCPenney. You'll see."

We arrived at a rusty metal ladder, identical to the one we climbed down. I looked at Thomas. "We gotta be chill about this. There could be people around the sewer up there." I pointed up. "Ladies first."

He shook his head, then climbed the ladder. I followed close behind. When we got to the top, Thomas pushed the cover up. It was heavy, but he could do it. Sunlight spilled into the sewer.

I squinted. "Is the alley empty?" I asked.

"Not a soul in sight."

"Cool. That'll make things way easier."

24

We climbed up into the alley and slid the manhole cover back in place behind us.

"There's Town Square," Thomas said.

"Exactly." I nodded. "And there's JCPenney."

We strolled over and walked inside, straight to the service counter. The manager looked up at us and smiled. "May I help you?"

"Yes, sir," I answered. "We're looking for a couple of suits, for a big party we're having."

He nodded and pointed us in the right direction. We wandered over, grabbing shoes, dresses, and suits as we went—and then we walked straight into the back changing rooms. The place was dead, and nobody paid us any mind.

"Michael," Thomas said, "we don't have the money for this. Where are we going to get it?"

I smiled. "We don't need money, Thomas."

I opened the door to the far right changing room, pulled him in after me, and dumped the clothes on the floor. Then I closed the door behind us and pulled up the corner of the carpet: another manhole cover.

"You gotta be kidding," Thomas said.

"Sure, these tunnels are in odd places, but they're damn handy for shoplifting."

25

The two brothers walked back through the sewers, back home, arms full of shoplifted clothes. Thomas walked back to his room. Michael sat down on his bed and began assembling costumes.

He'd shoplifted clothes from the dressing rooms of JCPenney.

Michael had committed his first act of crime.

II

1

I spent the rest of the weekend making disguises. After a hectic couple of days watching my friend's house burn to the ground, ducking through putrid sewers, and feeling the wrath of a religious fanatic, it was a nice change of pace. For the first time in a week, I felt I could finally relax.

That ended Sunday afternoon.

2

I was in the middle of listening to some music in my room, cutting some cuffs off a man's suit, putting everything into boxes for the team, when my door swung open and my mom stepped in, her eyes black with rage.

"I told you to knock!" I yelped, scrambling to hide my things.

"Where were you this morning?" she asked.

"I was here doing homework. You think I was out partying?"

"I told you yesterday to go to confession." She checked her watch. "It's noon. This is the Sabbath, Michael. Commandment Four."

Time to figure out what I wanted written on my headstone.

"Look, Mom, I'm sorry I didn't go today. It just slipped my mind—."

"It *slipped* your mind?"

I rolled my eyes. "Anything can sound bad, if you

put it that way. Look, it was an honest mistake. I screwed up. Can you just forgive me? Move on?"

She clenched her fists. She did this sometimes, and it just freaked out. "No." She shook her head. "I don't forgive insubordinate blasphemers who don't go to church—blasphemers like you."

"Really? I thought I was a 'child of God?' More to the point: One of the few things I've learned from church is that you should forgive. Always. Forgive me, Mother, for I have sinned. Sound familiar?"

"If you wanted forgiveness, Michael, you should've gone to church. But you don't. You just sit here." She waved around at my room. "Sit here and decompose in this basement."

"While you decompose your mind in church," I snapped. "You think worshipping two ghosts and a thirty-year-old virgin is a good way to waste a perfectly good weekend morning?"

"Don't you spout off at me!" she shouted. "You're *lost*, Michael! You still believe in God—." She paused and took a breath. "I can tell you do. You just need guidance."

"If you wanted me to go to church that bad, why don't you just wake me up for it?!"

"It's not *my* responsibility to get you there, to have you learn the glory of our savior. You need to *want* to know God for yourself."

"Your God is a lie," I said calmly. "And I didn't learn that from reading the books you forbade us from reading; I learned that from you. How's it worth believing in God if he just gives me your abusive, hypocritical ass?"

And then she slapped me.

I was speechless.

She'd never hit me before.

She looked at me, her eyes wild.

Then she seemed to get control of herself.

"You're grounded," she whispered. "For a month. You're going to wake up every day and use the confessional upstairs. Hear me? Don't ever let me catch you saying anything like that again. I swear, you won't leave this house until you're eighteen."

"What?" I shouted, regaining my voice. "'*Swear*?!' Swear on your false idol? Ha! I'll never set foot in a church for as long as I live!"

She clearly didn't give a fuck.

She just turned around and went back upstairs. I growled, kicking my bedpost in frustration.

"Fuck you! Fuck you! Fuck you! FUCK YOU!"

My phone rang. It was Kat.

"Hello?"

"Hi, Michael."

"Hey," I responded, still pissed.

"Something wrong?"

"No." I cleared my throat. "Nothing." I tried to sound cheerful. "Everything's good."

"That's bullshit, but I'll drop it."

"Thanks."

"I was screwing around on my computer this morning, and I thought of something. Couldn't look into the Dairy Queen's employees and their schedules? That way, we could collect the Dilly Bars when lazy employees are working. Make the whole thing easier. How's that sound?"

"Sounds good. I assume you already did it?"

"'Course. So there'll be several different options we could do, with some little extra work here . . . ."

While Kat talked, my mind drifted.

Mom.

She didn't care what I had to say. She wouldn't hear me out. It made me boil with rage, made me want to go upstairs and scream and . . . and *do* things. Bad things.

". . . Michael? You listening to me?"

"Sure."

"You're the worst liar. What you so pissed about?"

"Fine. My mom and I had a fight. Again. She thinks I need to be going to do confession more often. I told her to fuck off."

"Classic!" She laughed.

I got annoyed. "Hey, this is serious! She hit me!"

The laughter stopped. "Jesus, really?"

"Yeah, really. What, you don't believe me? Think I'm lying?"

"Like when you told me you were listening on the phone right now?"

That stopped me.

I didn't say anything.

"Michael, chill." Kat's voice was kind. "Sorry. I just wanted to talk about the employee schedule. The plan, right? *Your* plan?"

She was right.

Dead right.

As always.

Beautiful, amazing Kat.

"Yeah." I shook my head. What was wrong with me? "Sorry for blowing up. Weird day today with her, you know?"

"Yeah. It's fine. Sorry you got hit."

I shrugged. "It was only a slap. Surprised me is all."

"Could we start over?"

"Sure." I tried to brighten up. "Planning for their employees sounds great. Do it. A little recon on the targets is always good. And I gotta get back to making these costumes."

"Gotcha. I think we're gonna make some money, Michael."

I grinned. "Oh yeah."

"And we're not gonna get into trouble."

"Nope."

I didn't think I was lying to her when I said it.

But I was.

3

Monday after school, I met my friends in the cafeteria again.

"You ready to do this, guys—?"

I stopped in my tracks.

Bastard was sitting with the group.

He noticed me and stood up. "Michael! My boy! How we doing?" He strode over to me and shook my hand. "I've got something to talk to you about. Let's head over here."

"All right."

I looked at the others.

They just shrugged.

We walked to another table. I wasn't going to

have his fake-ass happiness. I knew he wanted something.

"Cut the shit, Bastard. So you wanna help with this? Great. What do you need?"

He nodded. "Getting straight to the point. I like it. It's what I do on the field." He flexed his biceps at me. Man, that fucker was weird. "I'll help you out if I get what they're getting—plus *half* of whatever you make on this."

I pondered for a moment. "If I say no?"

He snorted. "Well, it's either you accept or I'm gonna tell my father. Superintendent of Normal ISD. Heard of him?"

"Think he'll give a shit? It'll just sound like a bunch of teenagers screwing around."

"Well, if my dad won't care, *your* dad certainly will. I can just call him up, let him know I'm a friend of his son's, tell him the tale, and listen to the reaction."

I seethed. "You're a asshole, dude." I sighed. "But fine. Whatever. I accept."

I had no intention of giving him half my money, but I needed him and there was no time to fuck around.

We walked back to the table and sat down. Everyone looked at me. "Ready to get down? Get dirty?"

Kat took off her glasses. "We're going into the sewers?"

"Sure."

Logan laughed. "That's your reaction? *Sure?* 'So, uh, guys, we're just gonna casually walk across town through the sewers. No big deal.'"

I smiled and shook my head. For a dude who had just lost his house, Logan was downright perky. "You act like it's the craziest shit in the world, Logan. But straight up: Can you think of a better way?"

Logan opened his mouth, only to find he had no ideas. He closed it. And then he winked at me. Damn, I loved that kid.

"See?" I grinned. "The only other option I can think of would be a car, but we can't really change in a car. The sewers are perfect. They provide a hiding place for all our stuff and no one comes down there. Yes, it'll be pretty bad at first. But we'll get used to it. And Thomas will bring some clothespins."

4

We walked to the nearest sewer entrance in the school parking lot. We carried our costumes in the coolers we'd use to store the Dilly Bars. Using a little bit of elbow grease, I popped open the cover. After climbing down, I gestured the others to join me. When we were all together and had our clothespins on our noses, we marched forward, determined. I looked over at Thomas. He looked back. We both knew this was it.

The big heist.

We arrived at the first Dairy Queen after about fifteen minutes. I handed Ryan and Bastard the first cooler of clothes. "You guys know what to do." Then I looked at Kat. "You know the schedule."

Bastard nodded. "Meet you here when we're done."

The four of us continued walking to the second

Dairy Queen. When we arrived, I handed Logan and Kat the next cooler. "Get to it. We'll pick you up at the end."

Then it was just Thomas and me.

"You ready?" I asked him.

"Yeah. You?"

"Pretty nervous. What if the cashier calls my bluff on my disguise or calls the cops?"

He laughed. "Michael, you've got bigger problems than a fast food worker noticing you're wearing a fake moustache."

"Sorry. New at this. Sure, I've shoplifted hundreds of dollars' worth of clothes, but $20,000 in ice cream? That shit ups the ante."

"Yeah? Maybe don't bet so much next time, huh?"

"Again with the common sense?" I scoffed.

But he was right, of course.

I know that now. He was right.

But it's too late.

Anyway, after a little more walking, we arrived at the sewer exit behind the last Dairy Queen. "I checked this one out. It opens in an alley in the back of the store."

"Good." He nodded. "Let's get started."

I climbed up the ladder to the exit. "You ready?"

"Let's do this."

5

Michael and Thomas opened the sewer cover and climbed out. Sweat glistened on their foreheads. They both wore hoodies. They entered the Dairy

Queen. It was four in the afternoon. The store was empty, save for one tired college student, bored out of his mind, aching for a beer. Michael went first, pulled two coupons from his pocket, and asked for two Dilly Bars—free of charge. The student walked over to the freezer, got the ice cream, and handed it to him. Michael left.

Thomas went next. He took two coupons out of his pocket. The student repeated the action, handing Thomas the ice cream. Thomas left the store.

Ten minutes later, a woman in a frilly dress and man with a bushy mustache entered the Dairy Queen. They too ordered two Dilly Bars each—and got them. Hours passed. More people came in and ordered Dilly Bars. They all used coupons. As the clock struck nine, the last customers left and the tired student clocked out, put on his coat, and left the DQ.

He hadn't noticed a thing.

Meanwhile, Michael and Thomas climbed back down into the sewer, all smiles.

They had over seventy Dilly Bars in their coolers.

It was just the beginning.

6

A couple blocks away, in the Normal City Police Department, it had been a slow month.

Though there was the excitement of a recent arson case, nothing else was happening. Officers were bored, either filling out paperwork or out on patrol.

The Chief of Police, Chief James Evans, did his

best to keep morale high among officers, providing frequent coffee breaks and constant assignments. "Come on, we can fix crime and poverty in this great city!" he'd chant. "Get moving! Donut break in thirty minutes!"

Officer David Hallow—a new guy in Normal, but with a solid decade of good work in downtown Boise—was munching on a leftover donut hole and playing Half-Life on his laptop. He'd already finished the day's paperwork. Coffee cups and napkins littered his desk. Hallow was about to beat the Nihilanth when Chief Evans walked into his cubicle, his arms full of papers.

"Morning, David," he said. He peered at the screen. "What you doing?"

"Oh, just playing a little game."

Evans laughed. "I don't know if you should be doing that at work, buddy."

Hallow looked up from the monitor. "I finished the paperwork I'm supposed to get done. I looked at my schedule for today, and I've already finished everything. I've got nothing to do."

"Glad to hear it." Evans plopped the papers down on Hallow's desk. "The newest reports, something different. You're gonna put your forensic degree to work on this one."

Hallow closed his laptop and began to read the papers. "What's this about?"

"You know the city law that Mayor Goldstein signed last year about sharing surveillance tapes with us? Something interesting happened at the Dairy Queen off Main yesterday."

Hallow looked back at the chief. "Why was I assigned this? Why not give it to Charlie?"

"Don't you like Dairy Queen?"

"I love that shit."

"Good. Because it's your case. You've got potential, Hallow. I want you to use it. Save the world one case at a time, eh? Leave the monster killing at home?"

Evans winked and walked out of the cubicle. Hallow swept the trash off his desk, spreading the papers out. The reports described an incident in which several people had ordered free Dilly Bars with free coupons—and that these people had done this about seven times in an hour, for five hours. They'd essentially shoplifted seventy bars total.

How is this a case? Hallow thought.

Unless . . . .

He picked up his phone, dialed the NPD Records Department. "Hallow, here. Would it be possible get tapes from all three Dairy Queen locations yesterday afternoon, please? No, this isn't a joke. Yes, I was assigned this by the Chief. No, I'm not joking. No—. Look—. Wait. Can you just get me the tapes? I'm at 113. All right, thanks."

He hung up and took out a notepad, mind racing.

Ice cream fraud.

The reason you become a cop.

He laughed out loud.

7

And the scheme worked, if you can believe it!

Played out just as I thought!

No one noticed a thing! Ha!

I climbed back down into the sewer and dumped the last two Dilly Bars into the cooler. Thomas joined me a second later.

"Hell yeah!" He slapped me on the back. "We did it! First day done and *done*!"

"That wasn't so bad!" I grinned. I picked up the costumes and shoved them into a plastic bag. "Let's go pick up the others."

We collected our stuff and walked the sewers back to the others' locations. We stopped first at Logan and Kat's entrance. They were climbing down as we arrived, treats in hand, going for their coolers.

"I don't think we got a lot," Kat said.

"God, our cashier was an ass." Logan shook his head.

I laughed. "How many did you guys get?"

"Around seventy-five," Logan said.

"Seriously? Guys, that's great. That's plenty. More than us."

We hit our last stop with Ryan and Bastard. They were picking up their stuff. Bastard looked pretty shaken up.

"What's wrong, dude?" I asked.

He looked up at me, then back down at the floor. Ryan walked over to us. "Nothing's wrong. He's just overreacting a little."

"To what?" Logan asked.

Ryan smirked. "We got up to the cashier, and Bastard here just stops and runs out of the building. Apparently, he thought he heard dude say, 'How can't I see you?' When he really said, 'How may I serve you?'"

Kat laughed. "Jesus, what a pussy!"

"Come on!" Bastard hollered.

I shook my head. "And how many Dilly Bars you score?"

He sighed. "We got about sixty-five."

I nodded. "That's fine. Awesome. Brings us to well over two hundred bars to sell." I grinned. "Not so bad, eh?"

"Agreed," Ryan said. "This'll be done in no time."

I smiled. "Let's get out of this shithole."

After a fast hike, we climbed up the school sewer ladder, but Thomas stopped me on the way to his car.

"I came up with a little problem with your plan."

"What's that?" I asked.

He scratched his head. "Well, you know how you printed all of the coupons at home? Mom and Dad are gonna notice the ink and paper missing. We're gonna need somewhere else to print the coupons."

"That's not—" I began, then trailed off. "You have a point. We can't copy them at a big printing place, that's an easy way to get caught." I had nothing. "Fuck! Guess I'm gonna have to think of something before tomorrow, then."

"I'll try to think of something, too." Thomas put an arm around me. "Don't worry, man. We'll figure it out."

Always the optimist, he was.

Turns out, our 'little problem' turned out to be a giant nightmare.

A nightmare from Hell.

8

We went home and I checked out the mailbox. It was normally full of bills and promotions and this time was no different—but something new caught my eye.

Need some printing?
Come to Ku's Fax Klan!
Open 9-5, Seven Days a Week
365 Days a Year!
No Holidays Honored!
Ever!

Now, this was interesting.

I was holding the solution to my problem. Ku's Fax Klan was a small local business; for sure it'd have way less security than something like OfficeMax.

I ran inside.

Time to draw up another plan.

But why didn't I see it then?

Who the fuck names their printing store 'Ku's Fax Klan?'

9

The next morning, Chief Evans walked into Hallow's cubicle and looked over the collage of information that he'd put together. Then he scratched his head. "What the heck? You think we've really got something here?"

"Not sure, yet," Hallow said. "Got an anonymous tip today."

"What'd the caller say?"

"Said he was eating a hotdog at the Dairy Queen on Main, when he started noticing the same two people in disguise going in, ordering, and then leaving about once every hour."

"In *disguise*?"

"Yeah."

"You mean like with fake clothes and shit?"

"Yeah."

"He give anything else?"

"Not then, but I got home yesterday to find a blank envelope in my mailbox. Unmailed." Hallow dug into his pocket and pulled out a couple of little pieces of paper. "Inside were these."

Two coupons for free Dilly Bars.

"That explains a lot," Evans said. "The fine print on this says, 'Limit two per customer per day.' Hence the disguises. Seems pretty crazy—for an ice cream bar, eh? You find anything from the tapes to support this?"

"Of course." Hallow whipped out his laptop and opened a clip he'd saved. "Took me a couple hours. But I know I'm right."

He clicked play. Two people entered the store and used the coupons to buy Dilly Bars. Hallow thumbed at the screen. "See this? The taller one's head is parallel with the entrance from the camera's view. See the robbery strip on the door-jam there? The shorter one's about two inches shorter."

Evans nodded. Hallow opened another clip. "This

is from an hour later." Again, two people enter, exchanging coupons for Dilly Bars.

"They're the same height as the other two." Evans nodded. "Is this the same for the other two locations?"

Hallow nodded. "Different people, of course, but they come in every hour—in different costumes."

Evans clapped Hallow on the back. "Good work, man. Good stuff."

Hallow grinned. "I'll keep an eye on this, see if it's gonna be a regular occurrence."

Evans smiled. "Good. We've got real crime to fight here."

Hallow saluted. "You got it, Chief."

10

I woke up Tuesday with a new plan for printing the coupons. I got ready and hopped upstairs for some breakfast.

Mom stood in the kitchen, guarding the cereal. She had an empty tequila bottle in her hand. "You're not having breakfast today," she said.

I stared at her. "What I do now?"

"The real question is: What *didn't* you do?" she asked. But she didn't wait for an answer. "You didn't go to confession yesterday—or today. Again."

This shit was beginning to sound like a broken record. I started to say something.

But I couldn't.

Strangely, I was scared.

What could I say to her?

Nothing, I realized.

Nothing would make her any less angry or determined to make me pay for my "sins." So I was nervous, but I also found it liberating.

I could say whatever I wanted.

Things couldn't get worse.

Or so I thought.

"I told you already, Mom. I don't want to go to confession."

She slammed the bottle down, and it shattered. Glass shards flew.

I stood stock still.

But she was calm, as if she hadn't just broken a bottle on the countertop. Coolly, she pointed the broken bottle neck at me. "Your sins have consumed you, son. They've possessed you. A child of God has fallen. Like a fallen angel. I'm going to have to exorcise you."

Yes, you read that right.

She wanted to exorcise me.

"*Exorcise* me?" I asked.

She'd said it.

I nodded. "Um, no thanks."

And I sprinted out of the kitchen, broken glass crunching beneath my shoes.

"Get back here!" she yelled. "I can save you!"

I didn't care.

I grabbed my stuff, out the door and gone.

11

I got to school and sat down next to my friends in the cafeteria, still freaked.

Logan snickered. "Michael, Halloween was months ago."

I looked at him. "What?"

"You're white as a sheet! And you're one of the whitest white boys I know. What? You wake up with spiders in your hair? Told you to get out of that basement room, man."

I shook my head. "Don't want to talk about it."

He chuckled for a little longer, before realizing I really was fucked up. He dropped it. "Sorry, man."

I tried to force a smile, weak as it seemed. "You didn't know," I reassured him. "Anyways, I came here to talk Dairy Queen. We're gonna have to do some new printing. There's this local outfit, near Normal city limits, south of here. If we infiltrate after our Dilly Bar collection for a couple nights, we'll be able to keep the heists afloat. You guys up for it?"

Everyone nodded, even Bastard.

I rubbed my hands together, pulled everyone close. "Cool. Here's the plan . . . ."

12

After school, we were at it once again. After filling a cooler full of Dilly Bars, my brother and I stepped back into the sewers, tearing off our wigs.

"All right," I said, "four more Dilly Bars than yesterday; a new high score."

"Let's keep the streak going," Thomas said. We collected the materials and began walk to Logan and Kat.

I shifted uncomfortably.

He looked over at me. "What? Hasn't it been a good day?"

"Well . . . ." I hesitated. "No."

"What happened?"

I shook my head. "Mom and I had a little encounter this morning."

I told him what happened.

"Jesus," he said when I'd finished.

"That's why I was so freaked this morning," I said. "I almost feared for my life, bro."

"She'd never hurt you."

I flared. "Maybe she'd never hurt *you*."

"You really believe that?"

"Yeah. This shit always happens to me. All the time. But you never get it. Ever."

"Cool it, man. Didn't mean it to sound like I don't believe you. I've seen it, and I'm sorry it happens. Maybe you should try being nicer to her."

"Oh, so it's my fault she's psycho?"

"No. But you almost died when you were a kid, man. She prayed over you. She thinks God saved you. She loves you, and she thinks God chose something for you. When she says you're a 'child of God,' she *believes* that shit."

"Me surviving tuberculosis was *not* an act of God, dude. She didn't have to give up her teaching career

59

to go into the seminary, learn Greek and Hebrew, spend all her time reading scripture."

"Again, not your fault, but she still did those things. There's nothing we can do about it now, so you might as well man up and live with it."

"'Live with it?'" I squinted. "She's waving a busted bottle at me talking about *exorcism*, dude."

"What do you want me to do about it?" Thomas asked. "It's completely fucked up—and I don't blame you for that. What do you expect me to *do*?"

I shut my mouth.

What could he do?

Thomas hung his head, sat down on the cooler.

"We're not perfect," he said. "And I know she definitely isn't. But I know that a part of her deep inside loves you, Michael. Maybe this is her way of showing that love. She thinks you're special, man. Made for special things. God's work. I dunno."

"That's fucking *ridiculous*—and you know it."

"Is it?"

"Yeah. It is."

But I'm not so sure anymore.

In fact, now that I'm sitting here—after everything that's happened—in some strange way, maybe Thomas was right.

13

We kept going, picking up everybody, then making our way to Ku's Fax Klan. Bastard was still a little shaken up but less nervous than the previous day. That was good news.

When we got there, Kat, always prepared, got her laptop out and started typing furiously.

"You got the security footage up yet?" I asked.

"Almost. My hotspot sucks down here. I'm gonna need to head up to the surface if we want consistency."

"Fine, just stay hidden." I gestured to Logan. "Keep watch. We don't really need many people for this part anyways."

"I wasn't going up anyways." Logan shrugged. "Kinda freaks me out how the place is called Ku's Fax Klan, but whatever."

"Maybe they're black?"

Logan laughed. "I doubt it."

"All right," I said. "Stay focused. Thomas, Ryan, and Bastard, you're with me."

14

After a short stroll to the printer store's sewer entrance, we climbed up the ladder and conveniently found ourselves in the men's room of the place.

"All right, guys," I whispered. "Lights on."

We left the bathroom and entered the main area. It was filled to the brim with paper, office supplies, and ink cartridges. "Everyone spread out," I said. "See if you can find either a large printer or the owner. Preferably the former."

I walked to the right, into the owner's office. Nobody there. But in the corner, I saw a big printer. It was a gleaming, bulky, powerful grade-A machine, big as a fridge. I opened it, set a DQ coupon flat on the glass, requested five hundred copies, and pressed "COPY."

The massive printing brick churned and hummed. The time it took for all the copies to spit out seemed like ages. Every second we waited felt like hours.

After about five minutes, the final copy popped out. My stomach settled. I grabbed the copies and walked out of the office.

"Guys," I whispered. "Let's get out of here; I got the copies."

My phone rang. I took it out and answered. "Hey Kat, what's up?"

"You've got company. Dude coming towards the entrance. Probably the owner. You need to get out, now."

"Got it." I stuffed my phone back into my pocket and ran out of the room. "Come on, guys! We've got incoming! Get back to the sewer!"

We ran into the bathroom.

As we were climbing down, I heard the front door open.

"All right, who the fuck's in here?" A voice came, raspy—like out of a B-list horror movie. "Where are you?" A pause. "Yeah, you better fuckin' run. You hear me? Get the fuck outta here before I put fuckin' holes in your skulls!"

I slid the cover shut, jumped down onto the cement. "That was close. Let's get the hell out of here."

No one had any objections.

I didn't know it then, but I'd just met my nemesis.

Eli Sanders.

Eli fucking Sanders.

15

We hurried back and found Logan and Kat.

Logan greeted us with a nervous smile. "Hey, guys. How was it?"

Bastard shuddered. "I'm not coming with you next time, Michael. That dude sounds seriously fucked up."

"Me neither," Ryan said.

"That's all right, Ryan." I nodded. "It's more suited for two people anyway."

I unzipped my jacket pocket and pulled out the thick stack of DQ coupons. "Here's the money!"

Bastard shuddered again. "Can we just go home?"

I just laughed.

16

After a long day, Michael and his friends parted ways.

They planned to resume their scheme the following day.

Michael had broken into a store and trespassed on private property.

Michael had committed his second act of crime.

III

1

Wednesday came and went without a hiccup. Just another normal day in Normal—besides our Dilly Bar swindling, of course. We hid them in our coolers under my back porch when we were done. It was a good place for the ice cream for the time being because of the twenty-degree weather of mid-Idaho February. Thomas made sure the coolers were racoon-proof.

Thursday was a day off from school, as was Friday. I spent the morning sleeping in. I was exhausted from three straight days of working; it was time for a day of rest. At noon, I lurched out of bed and took a shower. I headed upstairs and got some breakfast.

"Morning, guys."

No answer. I stopped peeling my orange and looked around.

There was nobody in the house.

Not Dad, not Mom, not even Thomas, who usually sat in his room listening to music.

Where the hell was everyone?

I thought for a moment. Maybe they left a message? I looked at my phone and realized that I'd got a text from Thomas:

> Hey, Michael. Everything is cool. Decided not to wake you. Know you were crazy-tired. We're at the ICU looking after Mom. Come when you can.

I set down my phone. "What the hell?" I asked aloud. I grabbed my half-peeled orange, slipped on a coat, and jumped on my bike.

When I got to the hospital I ran up to the nurse at the front desk. "Where's Abigail Evans?"

He looked up at me. "I'm sorry, her family doesn't want visitors at this time."

"I am her family. I'm her son."

"Sir, how am I supposed to know that you're her—."

"Her husband is my dad, James Evans. The Chief of Police? My brother's name is Thomas Evans."

He looked at his computer. "They're in Intensive Care. Room 19."

"Thanks." I ran past him.

When I entered the room, Thomas and Dad were sitting by Mom. She was unconscious in bed.

"Get your rest?" Thomas asked me.

"How am I supposed to sleep when Mom's in the hospital. What happened?"

My dad was upset. "She woke up screaming at three in the morning and couldn't fall back asleep. Around five, she started screaming again, shouting, 'The fire! The fire! I can't save him! I can't save him! I want to die! I'm gonna kill myself! Can't save him from the fire!'"

I said nothing. I looked down at the tile floor. On one hand, I didn't have any sympathy for my abusive mother. On the other hand, well—she's my *mom*, you know?

We stayed there for a while, and then I left. It was weird, but I could tell that neither my dad nor my brother wanted me there. I don't know now why I felt that way, but that's how I felt, so I turned around and marched out.

I hate hospitals anyway.

"Nice way to spend a morning," I muttered.

But things were about to get worse.

Way worse.

2

By 4:00 PM, the gang was back at their respective Dairy Queens, collecting Dilly Bars. Thomas and I, other than a few grunts, didn't talk. Guess we had a lot to think about, and most of those thoughts involved Mom.

We climbed up to the Dairy Queen in our business suits and waited in line.

I didn't notice the man in the corner looking at me.

3

For the fourth time that week, Michael and Thomas left the sewers without a word. It was 4:30 PM. They'd collected twenty Dilly Bars and were on track to collect the most they'd ever collected in a day. But they were bored, their costumes were itchy, and with everything going on at home, they wanted to quit.

It was the tenth time up, when disaster struck.

Thomas had gone first and requested two Dilly Bars. The lady at the counter fetched the two treats.

Then it was Michael's turn.

He placed his order and received it with no suspicion, even though he was dressed as a woman.

He hurried to the door—and then a counterfeit Dilly Bar coupon fluttered to the floor from where he'd stashed it in his bra.

Michael reached down and tried to pick it up.

But a man beat him to it. He wore a police badge under his sweatshirt. "I believe this is yours," the man said politely.

Michael froze, collected himself, then said in his best female voice, "Why, yes. Thank you, officer."

He held out his hand.

The cop examined the piece of paper. The words "DAIRY QUEEN - GOOD FOR TWO DILLY BARS" caught his attention. "What's this?" he asked.

Michael began to sweat profusely. "It's a coupon. For Dilly Bars."

"Didn't you already use one?"

"I have two. I'm an avid coupon collector. Every Sunday, I sit down with all of the week's newspapers and begin snipping away." Michael smiled his prettiest smile. "Saves a lot of money."

The officer's eyes narrowed. He handed back the coupon. "All right then. Good day, ma'am."

The cop walked away.

Michael nodded and walked out of the store.

When he was out of sight of the Dairy Queen, he sprinted back to the sewer entrance.

4

I practically jumped down. I'd never been so scared in my life. When I got down, I suddenly puked—

everything, my breakfast, my lunch, anything in between.

Thomas patted my back. "Christ! You okay?"

I shook my head. My body convulsed. I felt faint. Writing about this now, I realize that it was probably delayed shock from seeing Mom like that in the hospital. But I didn't think about that then. Thomas grabbed his water bottle and handed it to me. I calmed down.

"Okay," he began. "What happened?"

I was panting. "This man—. I dropped a coupon. He asked me about it. I don't know if he was a police officer or not, but . . .. I'm scared anyway that he's gonna tell somebody. Jesus, Thomas, I'm scared. We're gonna get caught. But what are my creditors gonna do to me if I don't pay up. Fuckin' Super Bowl. I'm stuck between a rock and a hard place."

"Hey, hey, hey," Thomas soothed. "It's okay. Things will work out. I promise."

I rolled onto my stomach, not caring if my face touched the ground. "I need to get new costumes," I blubbered. "That guy saw right through me. I don't know if I can do this anymore."

Thomas rubbed my back.

We both stayed there for a while, until I finally I'd pulled myself together.

"I'm okay now," I whispered.

That had been my first scare.

Little did I know I was going to have more.

Oh, so many more.

5

Hallow busted through the police doors early Friday morning, eager to unveil his findings, and made his way to Officer Evans' secretary. "I'd like to see the Chief."

The guy didn't look up. "Chief is busy at the moment."

Hallow frowned. "Look, this is an emergency. I need to talk to the Chief right now. Could you tell him I'm here, please? Tell him it's Hallow."

The man stared at him. "I know who you are, Hallow." Then he picked up the phone. "Chief, Hallow wants to talk to you. Urgently. Should I let him in?"

A pause. "Yes."

Hallow walked into the office. The Chief sat in his chair typing, coffee cups stacked to the ceiling. The bags under his eyes seemed heavier than usual. "Sit down, David." He didn't look up. "What you got for me?"

Hallow began quickly. "I went to one of the Dairy Queen locations yesterday afternoon, taking field notes on the case. The two troublemakers were at it again. I even interacted with one of the suspects when he dropped an extra coupon—he was clearly distraught. Checked the surveillance for the last couple of days. They've been going there every day, from three to nine, collecting about seventy or so bars a day. The other two restaurants, the same thing. They'll be ten grand in the black by April, assuming they keep their pace." He paused. The chief was still typing. "You all right, Chief?"

The Chief closed his laptop. "Yeah, I am." He rubbed his eyes. "Sorry. Didn't get much sleep last night."

"What happened?" The question was out of his mouth before he thought about it.

"My wife." The Chief shook his head. "She was never perfect—my youngest and her have a strained relationship. Been escalating these last few weeks. Took her into the ICU after some suicidal behavior last night." He finished off another cup of coffee, made to speak, then shut his mouth.

"Jesus, Chief." Hallow frownedhe. "I'm sorry . . . . I wouldn't have just barged in if I'd known."

Evans waved his words aside. "I'm fine. Just a little shaken up. What else you got?"

"Okay." Hallow pulled out a photo. It showed a woman in a frilly dress. "After the Dairy Queen encounter, I went home and hit another lead. Know the case we dropped on Tuesday? About the Cantons' house burning down? These two cases could be connected." He set down a yearbook photo. "The son, Logan Canton, matches the description of one of the DQ suspects." He paused. "It makes perfect sense—being desperate, he must've rounded up some of his buddies and shoplifted Dilly Bars to get a down payment ready for a new place or something. Why they chose this way, I don't know. But it's motive."

"That your best lead?" The Chief raised an eyebrow. "Kids stealing ice cream to buy their buddy a new place?"

Hallow nodded, conceding the point. It sounded bizarre.

"Don't know," the Chief mused. "They seem unrelated. But it's better than nothing. You've got the possible connection with the Canton boy. Tell you what, I'll send an officer to talk to Canton about it. You keep digging. How's that sound?"

Hallow stood up. "Can do, sir."

6

In total, we collected two hundred and twenty Dilly Bars that Thursday. It was a good haul, especially considering my meltdown.

"Chill, Michael," Logan joked. "You were just caught cross-dressing is all." I grinned and punched him lightly.

Man, I miss that kid.

When we were together again, I made a last-minute announcement. "All right, guys. After we're done talking, I'm gonna make a last-minute stop. Gotta shoplift some new clothes."

Ryan rolled his eyes. "You're overreacting, dude. Let's pretend that dude *was* a cop. What's he gonna care that some idiots are getting a few extra Dilly Bars, huh?"

I shook my head. "Better safe than sorry. Thomas, you comin' with me?"

He nodded. "Yeah, sure."

"Great. All right, see the rest of you tomorrow. Kat, make sure all the coolers get to my back porch."

Kat gave a thumbs up. "Got it."

They all headed up and out of the sewers.

I turned to Thomas. "Let's get this over with. Fast."

7

After an hour of getting new clothes, we decided to go home. I took a quick shower and headed upstairs for some food. Dad was watching TV. "'Sup, Dad."

"Hey, son," he responded. His voice was tired.

"Mom still at the hospital?"

He shook his head. "She's been moved to the Bosch Mental Health Center—we don't know for how long."

I looked at the cold spaghetti I was fixing. I love Mom's spaghetti. But suddenly, I wasn't hungry. "Sorry for being annoying and emotional at the hospital."

Dad shook his head. "I know she hasn't been the best with you." He sighed. "That said, she's your mom. And she loves you."

"She nuts," I said without thinking.

He paused. Then nodded. "Guess I never really realized until yesterday how truly strange things have been between you." He paused. "It's easy to think that Jesus wouldn't approve of her fanaticism, her behavior. But you think he'd approve of your unwillingness to forgive her?"

I turned away. "You're just taking her side."

"That's not it, Michael. Not at all. Holding a grudge long after she's realized her faults—it won't solve a thing."

I turned back toward him.

He looked me in the eye. "All I'm asking is that you give her a chance. Would you do that for me?"

I looked at the floor.

Maybe he had a point.

Of course he did. I know that now.

But then, at that moment, I didn't know. Should I give her a chance? I looked back up. "Sure." I nodded. "And if she pulls this exorcism shit again?"

He stood up and walked to the basement stairs. "Come with me."

I followed, puzzled. Standing in the basement living room, he reached down, pulled a seam of the carpet up from the center of the floor, revealing a trapdoor there.

"Whoa," I muttered. "What's that?"

"You'll find out." He opened the trapdoor and climbed down a narrow ladder into a little cubby before inviting me to join him. Once I was in, he opened a little metal door and tugged at a chain dangling from the wall. A bare lightbulb flicked on. It was a thirty-square-foot bunker, about four feet tall. The sides were lined with rows of supplies, guns, ammo, canned food, and even a little stovetop in the corner.

I didn't know it yet, but I would get used to the sight of that little room.

"So." He grinned. "How's this?"

I gazed at everything in wonder. "This is really cool, Dad. Didn't know you were a crazy survivalist."

"Crazy like a fox." He nodded. "Had the contractors put it in when we were building. If you ever feel threatened or unsafe—if anyone tries to hurt or pressure you, just hop down here. She doesn't know about this place. You'll be safe."

"Hopefully I'll never need to come down here," I said. "I'll try to keep an open mind. I want her to get better."

"Good," my dad said.

We hugged.

It felt good.

It felt so good.

Why am I such a fuck-up?

8

Friday went smoothly. It helped that we had new costumes. Two hundred and fifteen bars were collected, a slightly smaller total, mostly my fault because I was more cautious than yesterday. Thankfully, I didn't see the strange cop, and no one asked any questions.

I woke up Saturday morning at 8:00 AM to my alarm and hopped in the shower. Once I was squeaky clean and free from sewer smell, I walked upstairs for some cereal.

Today was going to be a busy day. It was the day I'd set to sell off the Dilly Bars we'd gathered. Over eleven hundred Dilly Bars, if you can believe it, just sitting in coolers hidden under my back deck.

Now, I needed to figure out *how* to sell them.

Once I finished my breakfast, I picked up the phone and video-chatted Kat.

"Hello?" she answered groggily, wiping at her eyes, then looking at the camera lens.

"Hey, it's Michael."

"I see that." She yawned. "What time is it?"

I raised my eyebrows. "It's only 8:30."

"8:30?!" she yelped. "Shit, Michael! Do you always get up this early on a Saturday?"

"Hell no! I had to! I have shit to do, homework to take care of, and Dilly Bars to sell."

She groaned, then flopped down onto her bed. She was so pretty in the morning. "That's right. I'll call the others up. Your house?"

"Nope. It needs to be somewhere more secretive." I scratched my chin. "But where?"

9

We all sat down around the circular table.

"Seriously?" Ryan asked, looking around. "The meeting room of your mom's church?"

I shrugged. "What? You wanna sit in the pews instead? Say a little grace before we begin? It's pretty safe, especially now that my mom's in Bosch."

"Nothing bad about being here," Ryan said. "It's just feels . . . ."

"Like, *wrong*?" Bastard said sarcastically. "We're sitting in the Lord's house discussing how to sell shit we shoplifted. What could be wrong about that?"

"We didn't shoplift anything," I said. "We purchased items with fake coupons."

"Important distinction," Logan nodded sagely.

"Indeed." Kat tilted her head.

Thomas laughed.

"Let's get down to business," I said. "We'll figure this out and try to get this done before the sun goes down. Got it?"

No one had anything else to say.

"Cool." I nodded. "Now, we need to sell quite a few Dilly Bars. They can't stay in my backyard. So, starting today, we're going to try to sell them every Saturday. Any questions?"

Logan raised his hand. "Yeah, how'd you say we're selling them?"

"I was thinking we'd sit out on the side of the road at busy intersections."

"Out there?" he gasped. "In this weather?!"

I snorted. "Come on, Logan. It's not that bad out."

Logan chuckled. "Dude—first of all, yes, it's freezing today. Second of all, no one's gonna buy anything cold. Third, no one is gonna open their windows to give some shady-looking kids money for a Dilly Bar!"

I frowned, even though I saw his point. "Fine. What do you propose?"

"We could sell them in bulk on eBay," Kat offered.

I drummed my fingers. "How would that work?"

"Easy. We pack the Dilly Bars in boxes of one hundred and sell them for $300 each. That would be enough for shipping and handling, and enough to pay back your creditors."

"All right. So we put them into boxes and put them up on eBay. What's to say we don't get any takers?"

"That's the only problem," she admitted. "It's certainly risky. But I'd argue it's a lot *less* risky than trying to sell them out in the cold . . . ."

"Let's go with Kat's plan," Bastard agreed. "It's way better."

I scoffed. "You're just agreeing because it means not standing outside all day."

"Know what?" Bastard nodded. "I'm proud to admit that."

"This sounds like the best idea," Thomas said.

"Unless we think of something else, I say we stick with Kat's plan."

I looked around. Everyone agreed. I shrugged. "I still have my doubts, but let's go with it."

Logan slapped his palms down. "Whoo! We're done already! Time to head home! Ha!"

"So be it," I muttered. "I'll see you guys on Monday. After school in the cafeteria. We're doing some more Dilly Bar thievery."

I leaned back and sighed before looking over at Kat. "Let's head to my place to figure out some details."

She smiled at me.

And that felt good, too.

10

The next week went well for Dilly Bar collecting.

That's all I really have to say, I guess. There wasn't any drama or attempted exorcisms or run-ins or house fires of any kind. Perhaps that's the best kind of problem: when there are no problems to describe.

I did, however, have another run-in with one of my creditors on Friday.

I was walking to my locker after school. The next thing I knew, two hands gripped my shoulders and jerked me into the men's room.

"Whoa, hey, Jesus!" I shouted, both in pain and in the hope that someone would hear me.

My assailant shoved me to the floor.

I looked up.

It was my most aggressive creditor, Eric.

He glared at me.

So I went on the offense. "What the fuck's wrong with you?!" I yelled up at him. "Think I'll be able to get your stupid money if you keep assaulting me?!"

"I don't give a shit how you're feeling, buddy!" he hollered, slurring. I could count on one hand how many times I'd seen him sober. "I'm giving you three more weeks! Got it?! Or I'll bash your fucking face in!" Then he turned around, stumbled out. "Piece of shit . . . ." he mumbled.

The door slammed shut. I lay there on the floor, stunned. I stood up, shaky, inspecting myself. Overall, I didn't look too bad, apart from a small bump above my forehead.

"Dick," I said to the mirror. Was I talking to myself? Then I shuffled out of the bathroom and made my way to the cafeteria.

"Hey, guys," I muttered.

Kat was the first to stand up. Then she frowned. "Oh my God . . . . What happened?"

"Eric," I sighed. "Eric happened. I'll be all right. He gave me a pretty good bruise." I reached up to feel it. "But you can't even see it. It's fine."

I clasped my hands together and tried to smile. "So we've got some more dough to collect. Then afterward, we've got some extra work to do. We ready?"

They said they were, but I could tell they were getting sick of the entire project.

To tell the truth, so was I.

11

After collecting another two hundred and forty bars, we met up again.

"All right, so we have some more coupons we need to print," I announced.

Everyone groaned. Bastard simply shivered. "Michael, are you really sure that we have to do this again?" he asked. "I'm getting nervous, dude. We're gonna get busted."

I rolled my eyes. "You didn't even let me finish. Only two people need to do this: Thomas and me. You and Ryan can hang out together like the lovers you are. Logan and Kat are going to work more on selling off the Dilly Bars on eBay. We still haven't sold off the supply from last week. Backyard's starting to get pretty full."

12

Soon, Thomas and I were walking down the yellow shit road, as Logan called it, to the KFK printer store. Once we got there, I opened the sewer cover and turned on my phone light.

"Stay quiet," I whispered. "We don't know if that nutjob is here."

"No shit."

I climbed up soundlessly. Thomas joined me. I swung the bathroom door open. We quickly tiptoed to the office, where the big copier sat.

"Keep watch out the front," I ordered. "We don't have Kat to back us up with her cameras this time."

I took out a coupon and requested another five hundred copies from the copier. They began churning out at a steady pace. I looked around the room—and a yellow sticky note caught my eye. I picked it up and read it:

Confront the fucking bitch Amanda before Tuesday

I frowned.

"Amanda?"

That name sounded familiar.

"Hey, Thomas?" I whispered. "Who's Amanda?"

He moved closer. The last of the papers spat out and the room fell silent.

"Amanda?" He stopped as he read the note. Then he grimaced. "Oh my God."

"What is it? Who the hell's Amanda?"

Thomas's expression turned dark. "Michael, Amanda is Logan's mother."

"No way." I shook my head. "No way this can be *Logan's* mom." I frowned. "Amanda's a common name."

"I know, I know . . ." Thomas admitted. "But if it somehow were her and the owner's got some beef . . . ." He trailed off. "Why, though?"

We sat there scratching our heads. "This's nuts," I said. "If it's really her, then what—."

"Hey, *assholes*!" A raspy voice outside the office yelled. "I *see* you in there, cock-munchers!"

"Oh, shit!" I yelped, snatched the copies, and

sprinted to the bathroom. I let Thomas go first into the sewer before doing the same.

But the dude didn't follow us.

He didn't even come into the bathroom.

Now I know why.

But then it seemed strange.

"Jesus," I breathed.

"No kidding," Thomas agreed. "We're not doing that again."

13

Six weeks later.

Do I really want to talk about what happened during those six weeks?

Fuck no.

Do you really want to know what happened in those six weeks anyway?

Maybe.

In short, I failed.

And it wasn't this spectacular, cinematic failure where the hero makes a big fuck-up and things collapse from there.

It was just little mistake after little mistake.

Picking off little pieces of success until you get to a point where your whole plan has collapsed, only you don't know when it happened.

Little mistakes, man.

Little mistakes.

Here's how it went down.

14

The morning after our second break-in at Ku's Fax Klan, I called Logan. "So hey. You know how Thomas and I went to go copy more coupons at that one place?"

"Yeah?"

"Right before we left, we found a note on the owner's desk. It was something about confronting 'Amanda' before Tuesday. Isn't Amanda your mom's name?"

Silence on the other end. Then, "Yeah. That's really weird . . . ."

"We weren't able to get anything else from the place," I continued. "Is it possible that your mom had some run-in with this guy?"

"That would be scary if it were true. But I doubt it. She just wouldn't hang out with a guy like that. You think black ladies be that desperate? Look at the name of his place, man? He's a fuckin' nut. A crazy-ass racist nutjob."

I nodded. "That's reassuring."

15

Dilly Bar collection resumed Monday. The piles of treats continued to pile up in my backyard. I grew increasingly anxious. No money was coming in.

"It's been almost two weeks," I said to Kat at lunch Thursday. "Nothing's been collected. We've been sucking up Dilly Bars just to have them stagnate like VHS copies of *E.T.*. When're we going to start getting some buyers?"

Kat shrugged. "I can't control when someone gets the urge to buy twenty-five hundred Dilly Bars off eBay, dude."

"This was your idea, you know?"

"And?" She raised an eyebrow. "I'm trying to find someone. I put it on Craigslist yesterday and Facebook, too. We'll just have to wait. Chill."

I slapped the table. "Yes. 'Chill.' And please take your sweet-ass time. It's not like I have greedy creditors breathing down my neck or anything."

Kat looked at me like I was losing my shit.

I probably was.

And Bastard had had enough. "Maybe we wouldn't be having this problem in the first place if you came up with a less moronic plan!"

"Shut up, Bastard. You should just be happy you're getting paid for this."

"Should I?" He held up his empty hands. "Do I see a check addressed to superstar Jim Ulrin in my hands right now? Do I?"

I stared at him.

I didn't want to accept it.

Bastard had a point.

But I'm stubborn like that.

So I stood up and left without a word.

16

That evening, Logan called in a panic.

"A cop came to my house today!"

Classic.

Things were already going to shit that day; this news didn't make it any better.

I took a breath and tried to be chill. "Okay, so what happened?"

"He . . . he knocked on my door and demanded what I knew about stealing Dilly Bars!"

"What did you tell him?"

"Nothing! I told him I didn't know about that!"

"And did you keep calm the entire time?"

"Yes . . . ."

"Well, what do you have to worry about?" I asked, trying to play it super cool. "It's not like he put you on a lie detector."

"But—."

"But nothing. You're fine, Logan. I guarantee you no one else is gonna come to your door."

17

Four weeks went by.

The once-constant flow of Dilly Bars had slowed to a trickle as the stockpile under my back porch reached mountainous levels.

Everyone's morale continued to drop. We weren't making any money. All that work—and nothing.

Eric and my other creditors continued to assault me in school, occasionally knocking me around in bathrooms or dark corners.

I'd already thought things were bad enough by Friday, five weeks after the Amanda scare.

But then things got worse.

Because that trickle of Dilly Bars stopped altogether.

18

That Friday, Thomas and I began to climb up the sewer ladder to collect more Dilly Bars. The pleasant sixty degree afternoon did nothing to temper our mood. When we got up to the counter, I did my usual thing. "Two Dilly Bars, please. I have a coupon."

The cashier shook her head. "We don't take those anymore."

I froze. "Why not?"

"Too much demand. We would've kept accepting them if corporate hadn't come yesterday to see how things were going." She shrugged. "Sorry, kid. You wanna order anything else?"

I dropped the coupon. "No," I choked before walking out. Thomas followed.

"Fuck!" I shouted as I jumped back into the sewer.

"Same," Thomas said.

I sat on a cooler and buried my hands in my face. "What kind of fuckin' plan was this? Why couldn't I have done something better, like . . . ."

I stopped.

An idea was forming.

"No use getting mad now," Thomas mused. He pulled out his phone. "I'll tell the others. You've got a week left to pay back your debt, so it's time to start coming up with something else."

"Yeah," I said to myself. "Something else."

19

The idea wouldn't leave me.

It took root, a parasite in my head. I was distracted by it, long after we all met up, long after I turned out the light that night to go to sleep.

But it wouldn't let me sleep.

I tossed and turned.

It was too alluring.

The only question now was whether I would do it.

Whether I *could* do it.

I decided that I would.

And that I could.

I got up and put on some pants.

It was midnight. No one in the house stirred except for Thomas. He was in his room, listening to his tunes.

I slipped on my shoes and opened the sewer cover under my carpet. Then I jumped down and began walking.

I reached my destination just after midnight.

I climbed up the ladder and up into Ku's Fax Klan.

The same cluttered floor space and dingy bathroom and messy office.

I grabbed the keys hanging under the counter, unlocked the register, and began swiping it clean. I then grabbed a plastic bag, headed over to the office, and ransacked everything of value: fancy pens, memory sticks, ink cartridges, the money stuffed in drawers.

Then disaster struck.

The plastic bag was nearly full.

I was sitting in the desk chair, humming as I rummaged through the last drawer.

And then—in the drawer—I felt a cold, metallic object.

I pulled it out.

A gun.

I'm embarrassed to say that I yelped and dropped it—CLACK!—the gun skittering across the floor to the dark office doorway.

I just sat there for a moment, shocked.

"God, I gotta be more careful," I breathed. I walked over to the doorway, reaching down to grab the gun.

THUD!

A big, black boot stamped down on top of it.

Something cold and metallic pressed against the back of my head.

Then a voice.

A voice I'll never forget.

"Give me *one* good reason why I shouldn't pull the fuckin' trigger."

20

"You deaf?" the raspy voice asked.

My head spun. The man's boots seemed to swirl with the gun, everything spinning. I felt the pistol press harder against my head.

"Yes, sir. Just give me a minute."

"You don't have a minute," he said. "You got ten *seconds*. Ten. Nine. Eight."

I was hyperventilating.

"Seven."

There I was, kneeling at the mercy of a crazed print shop owner who I'd been robbing for weeks.

"Six."

Why on Earth did I bet $20,000 on some stupid football game?

"Five."

How the fuck did I think shoplifting Dilly Bars was the best way to get the money?

"Four."

Why couldn't I have gotten along with my mother?

"Three!"

And most importantly, why did I sneak out to rob someone aware of our previous break-ins?

"Two!"

I supposed none of that mattered then.

"Wait! Wait! Don't shoot!" I cried. "Look—I can make you some good money. Really, really good money!"

The gun didn't move.

"Right," the raspy voice scoffed.

"No! No! It's the truth! You'd be able to tell if I lied, right? You seem like—like an *intuitive* person!"

"Eh?!" The gun shook a bit, like he wanted to do it, like he wanted to pull the trigger.

I groaned. "Jesus . . . . Look, I have a gun pointed at the back of my head. I can't think."

"You're making your life shorter, asshole!" he interrupted. "Now stand up!"

I did as I was told. He closed the door and shoved me into the chair. I looked up.

He looked like a lumberjack gone mad. Black, beady eyes. Biceps thicker than my head. His black, goat-like hair looked as if he hadn't taken a shower in weeks and his scraggly beard didn't look much better. In the halogen light off the street, his eyes glowed like the eyes of a demon.

"So." He kept his gun pointed at me. "What makes you think money's what I want? What if all I want is to see your body sprawled over my living room carpet? Ooh, that would be a fucking beautiful sight . . . ."

I took a deep breath. No matter how much he smiled, he always looked crazed.

I asked, "What use am I dead?"

He laughed. "At least you wouldn't be stealing from me."

He suddenly stopped. A faint noise came from the bathroom. The man backed up and grabbed a shotgun hung beneath a shelf on the wall. He racked a round and pointed it at the door.

The door swung wide open.

It was Thomas.

"Get out of here!" I yelled.

Then he noticed the shotgun pointing at his chest and stopped, his hands going up automatically.

The crazy dude smiled, his black eyes twinkled, and motioned Thomas towards the chair next to me. Then he got out a roll of duct tape and put a strip over Thomas's mouth. Then looked at me. "This idiot with you?"

No point lying. "Yes."

Thomas widened his eyes and started to muffle loudly. The man pointed the shotgun right at his face. "Shut the fuck up."

Thomas shut up.

"Good." The man continued. "What're your names?"

I answered. "I'm Michael Evans, and my brother's name is Thomas Evans."

"Gentlemen, I'm going to say this once and once only. My name is Mr. Sanders, and that's all you're going to know about me. Know that your life will be short-lived should you attempt to fight back. Know that you won't see the next sunrise should I find you've been plotting against me. Know that I know you've been leeching off my store. Know that I want compensation! Know that you're gonna pay me a hundred *grand* by the end of the month. You hear that? Two weeks. Or else I'll slit your fucking throats. Your whole family and whoever else is helping you. I own you. I own your souls. Think about it like this: As far as you're concerned, I'm the devil himself."

Mr. Sanders opened the door, gestured towards the bathroom, and smiled. "Get the fuck out of my sight." Then his smile got bigger. His teeth were very long and white. "Nice doing business with you."

We rushed out. Once we were down in the sewer, Thomas ripped the duct tape off his mouth. "Are you *kidding me*?"

It's like I said at the beginning.

Fucked.

21

"I don't get it, Michael." Thomas shook his head. "Burglary now? You know stealing a gun in Idaho is a felony?"

"You're not helping," I said. "Why'd you follow me, anyway?"

"Why'd I *need* to follow you?"

"You didn't."

"Yes, I did. Clearly. Had the strange idea you'd end up doing something stupid and killing yourself."

"Yeah?!" I hollered. "But we owe him a hundred grand 'cause of *you*!"

He laughed. "Oh really? Explain that one to me."

I opened my mouth, then shut it. I had nothing. "Look, I'm sorry. I'm sorry I snuck out. I don't blame you. I know I got us into some deep shit, but I need your help to get out." A pause. "Again."

Thomas didn't say anything for a moment. When he did, it cut deep. "What if, one of these days, because of shit like this, I don't wake up in the morning, Michael?"

"You said you'd help me—."

"I agreed to help get *Dilly Bars*, bro. I didn't agree to have a shotgun pushed into my duct-taped face by some hellish timberman gone *loco*. See the difference?"

"Yeah." I looked down at the floor. "Don't wanna tell the crew about it. That's kind of why I need you . . . . You can hate me if you want, man. But you gotta help me tell 'em. You don't have to bother saving me anymore. You can even have the other half of my share if you want. I just need your help to get us out of this mess."

After another pause, he nodded. "Fine." He stuck out his hand.

And I shook it.

He believed me.

He believed *in* me.

And now look where he is.

I'm so sorry, Thomas.

22

I woke up with the sun shining in my face. I groggily looked at my phone. It was 10:58 AM. I threw off my blankets and got up. There was no reason to waste a Saturday. Once I showered, I hopped upstairs for my usual breakfast routine.

Mom was sitting at the table, reading the paper like nothing had happened.

I stood for a moment, gaping. "You're . . . out?"

She looked at me then stood up and wrapped her arms around me. "I am. I'm so glad to see you! Oh, thank the Lord!"

I kept my hands to my sides.

I was nervous to hug her.

"Mom . . . . Could you please let go of me?"

She backed off, wiping away tears. "Sorry."

I leaned against the counter. "So you know why I don't want you to touch me?" I asked.

She nodded. "Yes." She fidgeted. "I know it's hard for me to control myself."

I raised my eyebrows.

"Very hard." She nodded. "And I know you've been pushed away from God—not by your own will, but by mine." She sighed. "I won't pressure you to go to church anymore. The Lord has a plan for you, Michael. I know it. I must trust in His ways—in His power. He will show you your purpose."

"Maybe it'd help if we found something better to do together," I suggested. "You know? Like normal mother-son bonding?"

She brightened. "Oh! I know! We should—." She stopped herself. "You know, maybe you should decide stuff like that."

I nodded. "Maybe I should."

I turned around and poured my cereal. I didn't want to sit there awkwardly eating it while my mom gawked at me, so I started bringing it downstairs.

". . . Michael?"

I stopped and looked back.

She averted her eyes for a moment then returned her gaze. "I'm truly sorry. I really am. And maybe you might not believe me now, but I hope you will later on. Things are in motion now—things that will change your life forever."

I gave her a smile. "I love you, Mom. I always will. It's been hard. But I love you. I'm just gonna get my head wrapped around all."

I slowly walked downstairs, feeling a little happier than I had in a long time.

I didn't really think about her words until much later.

23

Back in my room, cereal in hand, my thoughts quickly returned to the Mr. Sanders "situation."

On top of owing $20,000 to some of the most impatient bastards to have ever walked this Earth, I now owed a preposterous $100,000 to a maniac with a penchant for violence and a hearty appreciation for the second amendment. What's more, I needed to figure out how to tell the others about the recent developments without getting browbeaten into oblivion. This was gonna be impossible, especially with Bastard.

"Fuckin' Super Bowl." I sighed. "Why'd I ever bet on that stupid game?"

There was no real answer.

So I spent the day unsuccessfully trying to come up with a plan and went to bed early.

24

My phone woke me.

"Hello?" I mumbled.

"What's up, Michael?" Logan chirped.

I sat up and stretched my arms. "Hey," I answered. "I just woke up."

"Jesus!" he exclaimed. "What are you, a hibernating bear? You even know what time it is?"

I looked at my wall clock. "It's three in the afternoon."

"And you don't find that the least bit disturbing?"

I rubbed my eyes. "Hey, if you need the sleep, you need the sleep."

He chuckled. "What for? You stay up late the other night? The Lovely Kat Lady finally succumb to your charms?"

"Sure." I shook my head. "Hey, I was wondering— are you free today? You know, to meet somewhere private with the others?"

"Oh, yeah, I get it!" Logan jested. "I get it, Michael! I know how much you want to suck on this big dick of mine, and I know you want to do it someplace special."

"Shut up," I laughed. "No, seriously. Can you meet up?"

His giggling died. "Yeah, I'm free today. What you want to talk about? Or you just want to hang?"

"I need to discuss something. Tell you when we get together. Would you mind telling the others? I gotta take a shower."

"Sure. Where are we meeting?"

I peeked out my window. "Looks pretty nice out today. Let's meet at the park by my house."

25

I ran upstairs after getting clean. Mom was on the phone.

"Yes," she said. Then a pause. "Yes, I understand."

A longer pause. I started opening a can of soup, wondering who she talking to.

"That sounds good. Okay, thank you. Have a good day." She hung up, leaned against the wall, then breathed a sigh of relief. "Good morning, sleepy head."

I grunted, pulling the tab off the can. "Who was that?"

"Church leadership."

I looked up. "What do they want?"

Her shoulders slumped. "Word got out over my

little trip to the ICU and Bosch. The church is not happy."

I wavered. "So are they going to let you go?"

She shook her head. "Far from it. They're sending me on a mission trip. To Haiti."

I froze.

This was interesting.

"What for?"

"So I can reconnect with God. Their hope is that it'll restore faith in the Church, help me get back on my feet. It's fully paid, round trip. It'll last six weeks, at least. And they'd like your father to come with as well. We leave Friday morning."

I struggled not to jump for joy. "Well, that sounds pretty fun, eh? Just you and Dad, spending some time?"

Mom smiled a little. "Yeah, I guess you can spin it that way. I'm just worried about leaving you, right after getting better and all . . . ."

"Leaving me? Nah." I poured my soup into a bowl and stuck it in the microwave. "If anything, it'd probably be good for me to get a bit more space."

"You'd be okay being alone with Thomas for a while?"

I put my hand on my chin. "I don't know . . . . He can be a real pain sometimes." I grinned.

She smiled back. "I think I remember him saying the same of you this morning."

"Yeah, right," I scoffed. "Speaking of Thomas, where's he?"

"Been in his room all day."

"Cool." I took my warmed-up soup. "Love you, Mom."

"Love you, too, Michael."

Once I was downstairs, the joy-jumping began in earnest, accompanied by hot soup spilling everywhere.

Thomas and I would be alone for weeks.

Alone.

Without parental supervision.

At that point, this is what I thought: Even though I was totally fucked, it suddenly felt manageable.

26

I quickly finished my soup and ran into Thomas's room.

"Come on. Get your shoes on. We're going to the park."

He groaned. "What for?"

"Crew's waiting for us."

He got out of his bed like a slug and got dressed.

"You're gonna tell them."

"Can't you at least help me, Thomas?"

"Sure. But I'm not gonna like doing it."

27

We walked upstairs and headed out the door.

"We're going to meet with friends at the park," I called out to my mom.

"Have fun!" she called back.

"You hear from Mom about their little trip?" Thomas asked as I closed the door.

"It's more than a little trip. It's almost two months!"

"Just in time, eh?"

I just about tore my own head off nodding so much. "Granted, we went from 'oh shit we're dead' to 'oh shit we're dead but with a little more time to try and not be dead,' but still—it's progress."

"If I'm being honest," Thomas said, "I don't think he'll actually kill us if we don't get him his money."

"Can you believe you just said those words, dude?"

He laughed.

But I was worried. "I don't know. Seemed pretty serious to me."

"Yeah, right. The dude's just a nut. I bet he'll just threaten you and then back off if we threaten to call the cops."

"That might make sense, if we hadn't broken into his store in the first place."

28

When we got to the park, the team was waiting for us, sitting by a tree. Didn't look like they were in the best mood.

"Hey, guys. . . " I began. "Where's the funeral?"

"Lay off, Michael," Bastard said. "There's not a lot to be excited about. This shit isn't working. And you know it."

I shrugged. "I'd imagine that I have more reasons to be glum, considering that I still need to pay back my creditors, and . . . ." I swallowed. ". . . Someone else."

Ryan looked up from his phone. "Someone else, Michael?"

I sat down. "Okay. Well. There's something you need to know. Something happened."

Everyone looked at me. Thomas looked at the grass.

"So after we parted ways Friday night, I got an idea. I was really desperate and really tired of being out of control, so I went over to Ku's Fax Klan, and—."

"No." Logan shook his head.

"—and I tried to rob him." I let that sink in. "And I got caught."

"'Tired of being out of control,' Michael!" Logan shouted. "That's your solution?!"

"His name's Mr. Sanders, by the way. And we owe him $100,000 in two weeks."

A second or two passed.

Then everyone exploded.

29

Hallow walked into his office Sunday morning, coffee in one hand, a stack of reports in the other. Another boring morning. "Why couldn't I be on duty today?" he grunted, sitting down.

A knock on the door.

"Yeah, come in."

The door opened. "How's it going, David?" Chief Evans asked.

Hallow gestured at the paperwork. "Morning, sir. Critical work here."

The Chief laughed. "What're you talking about? Looks like a blast to me."

"Oh, yeah."

The Chief nodded. "So David, I've got something to share with you." He was carrying a manila folder.

"What's up?"

The Chief sat. "I'm going away for a while."

"Something wrong?"

"What? No." He waved his hand. "Nothing's wrong. I'm going on leave for a few weeks to Haiti with my wife."

Hallow sat up. "Whoa, Chief! This is great!" He grinned. "A little time together, eh? Why you going to Haiti?"

"Service project. My wife's church is sending her on full pay. They want me with her."

Hallow nodded. "Hey, Haiti's at least warmer than here. When are you leaving?"

"Friday."

"You told anyone else?"

"No, not yet. I'll bring it up with the Mayor this afternoon."

"Why didn't you tell me sooner?"

"Didn't know sooner. Just found out yesterday."

"Shit," Hallow said. He scratched his head. "Wait— why'd you tell me first?"

The Chief smiled. "That's exactly why I'm here."

He opened the folder, grabbed a sheaf of paper, and set it in front of Hallow. It was a contract for temporary assignment of duty. "You're going to be our interim police chief."

It took Hallow a minute to process.

"Me?"

"No. Your desk." The Chief grinned.

"But . . . *why*?"

"You've got a decade of experience, you served as interim chief for Brody over in Boise, and you're of appropriate rank."

"What?"

"You show potential," the Chief assured him. "And if you're going to move up here, you're going to need some administrative experience in this station."

"Well—."

"And, hey! If you find you're not up to snuff, then you can step down and let Doller take it."

Hallow thought for a little longer, then stood up and shook the Chief's hand. "I accept. I promise I won't do anything stupid while you're gone."

"You'll do fine. Oh yeah. That reminds me. Remember that Dairy Queen thing from a couple of months ago?"

Hallow nodded. "Yeah. Dumb case. I looked at the security footage for one of the locations yesterday. They weren't there. What about it?"

"Well, it's good they weren't there. I dropped it last week."

Hallow shrugged. "Kind of stupid anyways." He looked down at the contract. "Should I sign this now?"

30

Eli Sanders opened the door to Ku's Fax Klan that morning, holding a half-drunk bottle of Gordon's.

Dropping his keys onto the desk, he took another swig.

He set the bottle down and prepared for the day. Printing until his fingers fell off from pressing buttons. It pissed him off. Yeah, it paid the bills, but he didn't like it. As he prepped the cash register, he looked up at the portrait of his father over the front door. The plaque read:

E.T. Sanders

Sander's Family Printer Store

Proud supporter of the NAACP

"Fuck you, Pop," he whispered at the picture. "'Everybody is equal,' eh? Shit drove you to your grave." He paused. "That *I* dug." He grinned mirthlessly. "Hope you enjoy the shop's new name, as well as my, uh, *policies*."

Sanders leaned back. "I'm working with a new client; did you know, Pop? His name is Michael. He's very cooperative. Well, 'cooperative' isn't the right word for it. More like 'threatened with death.' But it's a start." Sanders belched. "He's got a special little dark friend working with him. A hardworking little fellow, he is."

He leaned forward. "And you know what, Pop? Michael's special friend is going to die. And you can't do a damn thing about it."

31

I sat and waited for my friends to stop shouting.

"How could you, Michael?!"

"Oh, why did I agree to help your dumb ass?"

"How'd you even get into that deep of trouble?!"

After a few more minutes of beratement, the shouting died down.

"You done?" I asked.

"What the fuck is wrong with you?" Ryan asked. "We somehow need to scrape together a hundred grand—that's one-tenth of a *million dollars,* mind you—for a complete maniac, and you act like you just stubbed your toe?"

"Now, wait a minute," I said. "Don't think I'm not freaking out, too, just because I can keep my emotions in check."

"Oh, shut up!" Bastard chimed in. "You're the last person to keep your cool! Want proof? You owe another hundred grand 'cause you can't think straight."

I lost it, got up in his grill. "And what about now, Bastard?! Huh? Am I keeping my cool *now*?!"

Everyone shut up. Bastard glared at me.

I sighed. "I guess not," I admitted. "Look, guys—I'm sorry I put this crap on you. I really am. I'm scared shitless of Mr. Sanders, too. But being scared and angry about it isn't going to make it go away."

"Sure it can," Ryan offered. "Can't we just stop? This isn't our problem."

Logan frowned, then he patted my shoulder.

I loved the guys for that.

"I wish it were that easy." I sighed. "But I don't

think the guy's stupid. He knows about us. He knows about all of you. He—." I paused. "He's going to kill us if we don't comply."

The shouting resumed.

Thomas was next to lose it. "Everyone! Shut up!"

They shut up.

"Thanks," I said. "Now, I'd argue that having a brush with death is motivation enough to pay off the debt, but I have a feeling I'm alone in that."

"Can I just address the elephant in the room?" Logan raised his hand. "Mr. Sanders' printer store is called Ku's Fax Klan. I'm black, bro. Ever notice? What happens when he comes for me?"

"Logan," I said, "if it comes to that, we'll be there to protect you. But it won't come to that. It doesn't matter."

"'It doesn't matter!'" Ryan elbowed Bastard in the ribs. "Hear that, Bastard? A white guy with a Klan store wants to kill us. But, hey! 'Doesn't matter!'"

"No, it *doesn't* matter," I said. "Because he won't touch Logan. We're going to pay him the money. End of story."

"How're we getting the money?" Kat asked softly.

I slumped my shoulders and sat down. "I don't know."

"Better start figuring that shit out, tough guy," Ryan said.

"I am. And it's good that spring break starts tomorrow. We'll have all week to figure something out." I looked down and started picking at the grass. "Anyone have any ideas?"

"I don't even know where to start looking for ideas," Thomas said. "I've never seen more than a couple hundred dollars in one place, much less a hundred thousand." He laughed. "Where can you even find that much in Normal, Idaho?"

Logan eyes brightened. "The depository."

Everyone looked at him.

"What?" I asked. I could've kissed him.

"The Normal County Depository. It has a lot of Idaho's silver stored in there. We could break in and steal some. Hundred grand, easy."

"Yeah, right," Bastard shook his head. "We're teenagers, and there's six of us. How do you expect us to break in and steal a shitload of silver without anyone noticing?"

"No, Bastard," I said. "It's possible. Logan, is that the building on the outskirts of town that looks like something out of the nineteenth century? Glass dome ceiling?"

He nodded. "Be easier than you think to break into it."

A plan was forming. "Now we're getting somewhere," I said. "I'll draft some plans tonight."

"Hey, we haven't agreed to do it yet!" Ryan hollered.

I rolled my eyes.

But then I realized he had a point. "All right, fine. You guys in?"

"Absolutely not!" Ryan said.

"And why not?" I asked.

"Because it's dangerous and illegal—way more illegal than stealing fuckin' *Dilly Bar*s! And we'd never have to do any of this anyway if *you* hadn't broken into the KFK!"

"Well, I did!" I shouted back. "So now you have to

choose between life or death. What's it gonna be, Ryan?"

He sighed, nodding slowly, but he was pissed. "Life. I guess."

Everyone else nodded. Bastard was more hesitant, but he agreed. Even though there was something else in his eyes.

I'd have to talk to him about extra compensation.

But, as it turned out, that wasn't it.

"Good. I'll let you know tomorrow what I come up with."

32

We got home a little while later. My parents weren't home; they were probably out prepping to leave Friday.

"God, I'm hungry," Thomas exclaimed.

I shifted. "Thomas?"

He looked back at me. "What's up?" he asked.

He slipped off his coat and started heading downstairs. I followed. "You didn't say much during that whole thing. How you feeling about everything?"

"Well, I'm not going to say I feel amazing about stealing anything more than a Tootsie Roll from the Seven Eleven. But I understand what needs to happen for us to get out of this mess."

I couldn't believe he said that.

But he did.

I smiled. "That's good."

We went into our separate rooms.

I continued speaking. "Thanks for backing me up—."

Then I froze, in shock.

"Michael? What?" Thomas ran over. "What's—."

We stared in horror at my laptop. It had been sitting neatly on the foot of my bed that morning.

Now there was nothing but plastic pieces and keyboard keys littered all over my floor.

Thomas shuddered. "You don't think—?"

"It's Sanders," I said. "A warning. I guess he thought we wouldn't take it seriously."

"Well, we did!" Thomas shouted. "What *else* might he be plan on breaking before we get his money?"

The words "our necks" hung in my mouth.

But I didn't say them.

"Don't worry about him," I said. "I'll talk to him. Make sure he doesn't do anything else. We can't afford any distractions if he wants his money."

He thought about that for a minute. "All right." Then he walked out of the room.

I sighed and stared at my computer.

"Sanders, you piece of shit . . . ."

I sat at my desk and began to brainstorm.

33

I was up and moving by nine the next morning, raring to go.

I called Kat. "Hey, what's up?"

"Not much. Eating breakfast. You figure anything out?"

"I certainly have. That's why I called you. Come

over to my house in a half hour. Call Ryan and tell him to get his ass over here, too."

34

I let them in when they arrived.

"Chilly morning out there," Ryan remarked.

I chuckled. "Yeah, well we're going back out in it."

"What?" He protested.

"Don't be such a baby," I said. "We won't be outside for very long. We're going to the depository."

"What for?" he asked.

"I'll tell you when we get there. We'll take Thomas' car."

We walked to my brother's vehicle.

Kat shook her head. "God, this thing's a piece of junk."

35

When we pulled up into the depository parking lot, I turned off the engine and faced them.

"We need the locations of the security cameras. Anywhere near the vault or outside, we need to know where they are so Kat can hack in and disable them."

"Does that mean that I have to go in there with you?" Ryan grumbled.

"Sure does, buddy!" I smiled. "Won't take long. I promise. I'll take pictures of the cameras on the outside of the building later. Don't wanna take too much of your spring break."

36

We hustled into the entrance of the County Depository and were surprised by what we saw. The building was massive, the ceiling vaulted more than a hundred feet up. Smooth white marble floors reflecting sunlight from the glass ceiling. To the sides, gleaming carved statues of mythical monsters and financial historical figures lined the walls, a strange mix. St. George and the Dragon right next to some guy named Junius Morgan. Didn't make sense to me.

"Jesus Christ," I said. "This seems excessive for a place to store some shiny metal."

"*Expensive* shiny metal." Ryan nodded. "But yeah. Why spend this much money on shit you pass by on the way to the expensive shiny metal?"

I nodded. "The guy who built it was the owner of several silver mines around Idaho. His name was Frank Heese."

"And why in the world do you know that?"

"I was doing some research yesterday on the depository. Name came up."

"You're weird."

"Shut up and take the pictures, man."

A few minutes passed of wandering around and snapping pictures of the ceiling and walls. I sent the pictures to Kat.

"Ryan, call Kat."

"Sure. I'll put her on speaker." He pulled out his phone. A second or two passed. "Hey, Kat. We sent the pictures to you. They look good?"

"Yeah. But I need more footage. I need to know where the cameras are near the vault."

I looked over at the far end of the hall. A guard stood in front of a metal gate, hiding the view beyond. "There's a guard in the way. We can't just walk in there like it's our place."

"But isn't it?" Ryan asked. "I mean, this is government land, right? Don't we have a right to tour it?"

There was a brief pause. "That sounds like a pretty good idea," Kat agreed. "I'm not saying it'll work, but it's worth a shot."

I shrugged. "All right. Let's try it."

Ryan hung up the phone as we walked over to the front desk. A middle-aged receptionist typed away at her computer. With barely a pause in her typing, she said, "Good afternoon, gentlemen. What brings you to the Normal County Depository?"

I cleared my throat. "Hello. We would like to tour the depository."

She still didn't look up. "What for?"

I didn't have an answer.

Ryan saved us. "We'd like to take a gander at its beautiful architecture. You know, learn of the history of the place."

The receptionist looked up and smiled. "Come along, gentlemen."

She stood and led us past the gate. The guard quickly screened us for contraband before letting us through. The large room outside the vault seemed to be quite a bit larger than the entrance hall. A giant glass dome gleamed with the spring Idaho sun. On the far side of the dome stood a large vault. It was tar-black with a giant wheel locked by several combinations. I walked slowly around the room. Ryan separated and walked the opposite direction. The woman watched as I gazed above, taking pictures of the ceiling and looking for any cameras. I saw two; Kat could find more if she looked at the footage.

The receptionist smiled. "Isn't it beautiful?"

I smiled. "Yes, it is, ma'am."

"Excellent. Why don't I start in the 1800s, when the Silver Rush was in full swing?"

"Ah!" I pretended to be surprised. I checked my phone for the time. "I am so sorry, but we need to get going! Appointment that we forgot."

The women shrugged nonchalantly, but I could tell she was disappointed.

"That's all right. Come along. I'll lead you to the exit."

We walked back into the hall. "Have a good day, gentlemen," she said.

I waved back. "We're done," I whispered to Ryan. "Let's get out of here."

I got into the car and started the engine. Ryan got in the back. Kat was staring at her laptop. After a pause, she closed it and smiled back at me. "I think we're all set. I'll take a bit more time looking, but I think we're ready to do this."

"Whoa! Slow down there," I said. "We have all week. I was planning to rob it this Sunday, when the place is closed and everyone's out at church."

"Oh," Kat said. "What are you going to be doing all week then?"

"Looking over the plan, checking to see if anything's off, getting supplies—you know, getting ready? Getting ready to be *done*."

Ryan nodded. "Not bad. I think I'd really like to start 'being done' soon."

37

As expected, the rest of the week was spent poring over the plans and gathering materials. It was pretty relaxing, really. After a shitty couple of days, planning something out felt pretty good.

Friday morning, Thomas woke me with a pillow to the head. "Yo! Michael! Time to get up. Mom and Dad are leaving!"

I got up, blinking. "Fuck me. What time is it?"

"Pretty early. 5:30."

"What? Why are they leaving that early?"

"That's when their flight leaves for Seattle, dummy."

"Boys!" came Dad's voice from upstairs. "Come up to the foyer! It's time to say goodbye!"

Thomas and I went upstairs. Our parents were waiting, luggage in hand. We all exchanged hugs. They were true acts of affection. I looked my mother in the eyes. She was smiling, but a hint of sadness hid there.

"You gonna be okay?" I said.

She nodded. "Yeah. I think so, anyways."

"It'll be good, you know. Good for the both of us."

"Agreed." She gestured upstairs to the kitchen. "We've left some money for you, when you need groceries or anything like that over these next weeks."

"Cool," Thomas said. "You guys better catch your flight."

"Yeah," Dad said. "Let's get out of here, honey."

They waved us goodbye and walked out of the house. We watched them drive off in the dawn light.

I leaned against the wall. "I'm gonna miss them. I'm really gonna miss them."

A sound came from the living room.

We looked at each other.

"What the hell is that?" Thomas asked.

The printer was processing something.

"What the hell?" my brother said. "A *fax*?"

"It's Mr. Sanders," I said. "He found our number."

"How do you know this is Mr. Sanders?"

"Who else faxes nowadays?"

The fax spat out. I picked it up and read it.

BRING YOUR CREW TONIGHT.
SEVEN O'CLOCK SHARP.

-MR. S.

"When is he going to leave us alone?" I groaned.

"I guess I'll give everyone a call later today, tell them they have to show up."

"Yeah." Thomas looked at me. "Good luck with that."

38

As I expected, the team was both nervous and pissed when I told them.

"What the hell does he want?" Ryan asked.

I shrugged. "I have no clue. You read the fax. He can't hurt us. Not if he wants his hundred grand."

"I didn't see *that* on the fax," Kat said.

"Well—."

"Then you don't know for sure, do you?"

I sighed. "I guess not. But you know what I *do* know? That Mr. Sanders will retaliate if we don't see him tonight. That I guarantee."

No one argued with that. I nodded. "Glad we're all on the same page."

"But, Michael," Logan said, "he hasn't met me yet. How do you know he won't, like, I dunno. . . retaliate right then and there? He's a racist pig."

I sighed. "You think he'll just attack you?"

"How do you know he *won't* attack me?"

I dropped my head, realizing that he was right. I didn't know what Mr. Sanders was going to do at all.

But there was nothing I could do about it now.

"We'll figure something out," I said lamely.

God, this is all my fault.

I thought telling you would make it better.

It doesn't.

I'm so sorry, Logan.

39

They started to trickle in around six. The mood was

tense. The last person to show up was Logan. He showed me a switchblade, hidden in his belt. "Just in case," he said.

We sat around upstairs for a little while and had a snack. Seven o' clock came fast.

"Come on, guys. Let's go."

We went down to the basement, entered the sewer, and headed over to Ku's Fax Klan. The group walked slowly, worried. I tried reassuring them, but it didn't really help.

And they were right.

I didn't know it then.

But we were playing his game.

From the very beginning.

40

We climbed out of the sewer and left the bathroom. Mr. Sanders was waiting, sitting on the end of his desk. There were some shot glasses set up in front of him. He made eye contact with Logan, but otherwise didn't react. His black goat-hair was wild.

"Good evening," he said calmly, once we were all up. "Come, sit down."

Hesitantly, we sat down in chairs farthest from him. He spread his hands at the glasses in front of us, then reached under his chair. "I have something for you."

Tequila.

"The only thing I had in my fridge that hasn't gone bad." He grinned.

Everyone shook their heads.

"We're underage," I said.

"So? Drink up! I didn't sacrifice my hard-earned alcohol just so you pussies could skimp!"

When no one moved, he looked over at me. "I think you should demonstrate to your friends what drinking is."

It wasn't a request.

He opened the bottle and poured me a shot. A big one. Triple-sized. Then he looked at me, waiting.

"Fine." I took it, chugged it down. It burned at first. I hated it. Then it became more tolerable—but I still felt nauseous.

Mr. Sanders looked at everyone else. "So who's next?" he asked.

You'd swear everyone had been turned to stone.

Sanders sighed. "Fine. Your loss, I guess." He took a long swig. "God damn, you guys're missing out on the good shit!"

"How 'bout you shut up and get to the point," Kat said softly. "We don't want to be here any longer than we have to."

"And I don't want to be talked down to by a little whore," Mr. Sanders whispered.

Then he blinked and looked at my brother. "You. It's Thomas, right? I assume you're second in command?"

Thomas nodded, giving Colonel Sanders a finger-licking death stare.

"That's correct," he said.

"So what's the plan? What's going on? How're you getting my money?"

Thomas looked confused. "Pardon?" He looked at me. I shrugged.

"I want to know if you have a plan for Sunday's depository robbery."

How did he know?

"At least, I hope it's Sunday; most places would be closed and everyone's at church. But since you can't answer a simple fucking question, I'm forced to turn to Michael. So, Michael, what good is your older brother in this heist?"

I cleared my throat. "He's quiet, quick on his feet, and will watch for guards or anything that might give us away."

"And the rest of these idiots?"

I pointed to Kat. "Kat will hack into the depository's system using her laptop to disable the cameras, while we take the silver. Ryan will open the glass panels in the skylight using special tools his dad had in his garage. Bastard, being the strongest, can carry a lot of the silver out with us. And finally, Logan here—."

"No," Mr. Sanders interrupted.

I furrowed my brow. "No? Why?"

Then Sanders threw his head back and roared with laughter. "Oh, that's funny. You think I'm gonna let this one work for me?"

"What the fuck you just say?" Logan asked, standing up. "What the fuck you just say to me?"

Mr. Sanders smiled. "Sit the fuck down, boy! Adults be talking!"

"Piece of shit," Logan whispered. He pulled his switchblade and moved forward, deadly.

I tried to stop him. He pushed up against me.

"You asshole," Logan said. "You cracker-ass, dogshit, sister-fuckin' redneck asshole."

Mr. Sanders' smile went bigger. And then he pulled a gun, a black revolver. "Guess we won't be working together. Hit the road. And take your monkey with you."

"You don't want your money anymore?" I asked bizarrely.

"Oh, you're gonna get me my money." He leered. "Just not with little black sambo running around with you. Next time I see you, you better have cash in hand, Michael. Or you know what'll happen. Now *get*."

We stood up, everyone confused, and went back to the bathroom. Logan's throat was hoarse with rage. As soon as we'd climbed back down into the sewer, we huddled around him.

"It's okay," Kat said, rubbing his back.

But everyone glared at me.

Their eyes spoke volumes.

You did this.

You hurt him.

They were right, of course.

It was my fault.

But it was Sanders who would pay.

At least that's what I thought then.

41

I woke the next day with a pounding headache and a dry mouth.

"Jesus," I muttered, wincing each time I moved my head. I got up and wandered over to Thomas' room. He was still sleeping.

"Thomas." I nudged him.

"Nggh." He tossed and turned. "What do you want?"

I groaned, my head splitting. "Come on, you gotta get up! Time to get ready for the heist!"

He sat up, confused. "Michael, do you know what day it is?"

It was my turn to be confused. "Sunday. At least, I think? I can't think because of this stupid headache."

"You know why you have a headache?" Thomas continued. "Because you drank a giant shot of tequila. And you don't know what else was in it. Whatever it was, your body didn't handle it well. And it's Saturday, dumbass."

"I have a . . . *hangover*?"

"Yeah, genius. Now would you get out of my room? I'm trying to get some sleep."

I shrugged then left. I went upstairs and took some aspirin. My day was spent going over the plan several times.

It was go time, and I couldn't afford to fuck things up.

Or maybe I should say: I couldn't afford to fuck things up worse than I already had.

42

Sunday morning.

I woke up to an alarm I'd set the night before.

I hopped out of bed and got ready.

The time was 7:00 AM.

43

Thomas and the others were already upstairs waiting for me.

"Damn, Michael. You get ready like a girl in the morning," Logan joked.

"Hey!" Kat said. She slapped him playfully on the arm.

I smiled. "Yeah, well, this isn't a typical morning."

Logan dropped his smile. Despite his best efforts, the mood was low. I didn't let it get to me. Like I said before, the burdens of leadership.

"So does everyone know what they're doing?" I asked while making breakfast.

Everyone nodded, though not with much enthusiasm.

Bastard spoke up. "Michael, what happens if we're caught? What happens if someone gets hurt?"

I knew I couldn't guarantee those things were impossible, but I had to convince him. "None of that's gonna happen, Bastard. I've gone through this plan enough times this week—I can recite it from memory in my sleep. Just calm down, keep your head in the game."

The conversation was over. I set down my cereal and stood up. "Let's get our stuff on," I said.

We put on our ski masks without a word.

The car ride was silent.

But my mind was screaming.

I'd gone from Dilly Bars to silver bars in less than a month.

My mom would be so proud.

44

We drove into the depository parking lot.

I faced my crew.

"We ready?"

A series of nods.

"Good. Now, from the moment we step out of this car until when we climb back into it, we'll be calling ourselves by the first initial of your first name. I'm M, Kat is K, Bastard is B, Ryan is R, Thomas is T, and Logan is L. Clear?"

More nods.

"Good. Now, let's get down to business. Kat, you covered the license plates before we left?"

"Of course."

The car stopped.

We opened the doors and got out.

We were about to become bank robbers.

45

M's crew stepped out of the car. K stayed inside. Adjusting their mics for communication, M, L, T, B, and R circled the depository, set up their ladder, and climbed to the roof.

"Watch your step, gentlemen," M said. He held his mic to his mouth. "K, you ready for us?"

"Almost done. Gimme another minute."

"We can wait." M scanned the horizon. "T and B, check our surroundings while K finishes disabling the cameras."

M slipped on some gloves. R handed him the drill and special bit.

"M, the cameras are down," K said quickly. "But I don't know for how long. You might have a ten-minute window. Hurry."

"Well, that was fast," R remarked.

"That's what your girlfriend said last night," L said.

K laughed. "Damn, R. L got you pretty good. All we need now is a B, an L, and a T and we've got ourselves a fuckin' sandwich!"

"Jesus," M said. He powered on the drill and started cutting a hole in the glass.

After a few seconds of clean cutting, a glass circle popped up. M set it on the roof. "All right, we're ready to climb down. L, we hooked up?"

M felt a hand wrap around his waist, followed by a short click. "Now you all are. At your command, M."

"We're ready." M nodded. "Lower us down."

One at a time, the crew slid down to the floor of the depository. T was the last to drop to the tile. The rope clattered to the floor.

"I know I've said this before, but *dang*," T said. "Why the hell is this in Normal, and not Boise?"

"Who the hell knows," R said.

"Stay on the lookout, guys," M said as he unbuckled himself. "R? Tools?"

"Yep," R said. He held up a briefcase. "Let's crack this thing open."

The three walked toward the safe. It was protected by three electronic locks. The other three followed closely behind. When they were at the foot of the safe, R opened the briefcase and took out a small metal device shaped like a keypad.

"So, uh, K? Walk us through it one more time?" R asked.

"Pretty easy," K said. "Open the two latches on the sides, stick it over one of the number pads like a plunger over a clogged toilet, then press the red button on the top. The machine should process the numpad and tell you the combination on the screen. Take it off, type it in, then rinse and repeat with the other two locks. Simple. But guys, the security system is threatening to lock us out in a few minutes. Move it."

"No sweat," T said.

R opened the latch on the hacking device and set it over the first keypad. After a few moments of processing, the digits 83720 appeared on the screen. Beep. Beep. Beep. Beep. Beep. The keypad lit up green. R repeated the steps until the final keypad lit up with a satisfying sound.

"Unlocked."

There were several clanking sounds from within the door, and then the circular metal door silently swung open. M, R, and T gaped at the treasure before them.

Silver bars.

Silver bars everywhere.

Jackpot.

M shook his head. "Enough gawking. Let's go!"

He ran in and started stuffing silver bars into his duffel bag. The others followed. After a few minutes, everyone's bags were full—and crazy-ass heavy.

"All right, let's get out of here," M heaved, slowly lifting the stacked bag over his shoulder.

They moved out of the vault and together pushed the door shut. It closed with a too-loud clang. M winced.

And then he saw the pile of rope on the depository floor.

"Hey, L," M spoke through the mic. "Our plan was to climb back up to the roof. What's the rope doing down here?"

"I—," L began. He made a clamping sound through the mic. "Shit. I didn't think of that!" L laughed, then waved down to the rest of them. "Why did I drop it?"

"We're never going to escape," B whispered. "We're going to rot in jail and never see the light of day again!"

"Shut up, B," M said. "I came prepared." He reached into his duffel bag and brought out a wad of plastic explosives and a little digital detonator. "Never wanted to use this, but it looks like we're gonna have to improvise."

"Where'd you get that?" B hissed. "What the hell!"

"Chill!" M snapped. "I made it yesterday. There was no guarantee I was going to use it—but I'm glad I prepared." Then he spoke into the mic: "All right—listen up, K. We're gonna blow up the front gate of the depository. Only way to get out. Park near the front, then be ready to drive, we'll take the interstate back to our house. Got it?"

"Okay," K answered, "but a little reminder? The system's gonna shut me out in less than a minute, and then a whole bunch of alarms are gonna go off."

"Oh, blowing up the front of the building is going to set off a whole bunch of alarms anyway," M grinned. "L, you're going to have to climb down the roof. The rest of you—come with me. B, grab that rope."

"You kidding?" T said as everyone headed over to the entrance. "*Destroy* the front of the depository?"

"Yup. I don't give a shit about Normal architecture, and neither should you."

"This is the best plan we have?" R asked.

M set down the bomb and started the timer.

"I mean, can't we just throw our rope back up to L?"

"Not unless you know how to hurl fifty pounds of rope a hundred feet in the fuckin' air," M said. "And we now have twenty seconds to get the hell away from this thing."

The four ran to the other side of the hall, covering their ears. Moments later, the little bomb went off. SHOOM! It felt like a small earthquake. A hole at the center of the front gate blasted open. Shrapnel shot in all directions. Wailing alarms screamed. WEE-OOO! WEE-OOO! Once the dust had settled, M shouted through the mic, "All right, guys! Get the hell out of there! Go! Go! Go!"

They ran towards the hole in the gate. K had the car in gear, ready to slam on the gas. L was already with her, riding shotgun. M scrambled into the back. R, T, and B dove in anywhere they could.

"All right, K! *Drive!*"

The Normal County Depository was on the far outskirts of town. Of the few people who lived nearby, most were out, attending church.

"Fuck yeah!" M cheered.

Everyone hooted.

"Hell yeah!" R laughed. "We're filthy rich!"

M had robbed a bank.

M had committed his third act of crime.

IV

1

Hallow and his team from the NPD arrived at the Normal County Depository collectively amazed.

"Gonna be a long day," Hallow muttered.

The Depository was in sorry shape. A hole the size of an oven gaped in the front gate. The interior was littered with debris. The glass dome on the roof was missing a chunk of window pane. To make matters worse, it was pretty clear that the safe had been cracked—and that silver was missing.

Officer Charlie walked up to him. "Well, this is pretty terrible."

"Tell me about it," Hallow agreed.

"We're gonna be dealing with this crap all day—and for the next year, easy."

An officer ran over to them. "All right, uh, Chief. Here's what we have so far: We originally thought there were only five people involved in this. But the team inside and on the roof discovered four sets of shoe tracks, with more pronounced tracks on the roof. We think that the one on the roof roped the other four down. However, there's no way the five suspects could've escaped fast enough without the surveillance cameras catching them. Taking both pieces of evidence into account, I estimate that there must've been another person in the car, a hacker. He drove and disabled the cameras."

"Thanks." Hallow nodded. "Work the scene."

The officer got back to it.

Hallow frowned. Six suspects, or at least it's presumed so.

Six.

Hallow's frown deepened. "Give me a moment, will you, Charlie?"

"Certainly, Chief." Charlie nodded.

"Thanks." Hallow took out his phone, dialed.

"Hey, Chief. How you doing? How was your flight? Yeah? Good. Hey, listen—need to talk to you about the Dairy Queen case real quick."

2

Everyone remained in good spirits as we drove into the KFK's parking lot.

"We're finally done," I said, slightly dazed by the thought. "Nothing illegal for us anymore. We're out. We made it."

"And no more dealing with crazy ass in there," Ryan pointed to the printer store. "Seriously, fuck Mr. Sanders."

We all laughed.

"Fuck Mr. Sanders!" everyone yelled in unison.

My face was a permanent grin. "As much as I'd love to stay here and listen to you guys roast the asshole, we need to bring the silver inside." I opened the car door and started hauling out the bags of soon-to-be money.

"You sure you don't want me to come with?" Thomas asked.

I shook my head. "Nah. He'll be in a good mood. He's getting rich today."

My brother nodded. "Alrighty then."

He turned back to join in the fun. One by one, I hauled every bag out, except one; that remaining bag I planned to use to pay back my bookies and, more importantly, my gang.

Mr. Sanders was standing behind the counter, fiddling with the cash register. He watched me bring in the bags one at a time, without saying a word. I finally dropped the last in front of him. "Here we go. A little over one hundred grand worth of silver."

He was strangely emotionless. After taking a couple of seconds to finish up what he was doing, he looked up. He didn't even look at the bags.

"This isn't what I asked for."

My heart stopped.

The whole world seemed to stop.

I cleared my throat. "What do you mean?"

He smiled and said softly, "I think you know what I mean."

"What?" I stammered, panicking. "I don't know what you—."

Then he casually pulled his revolver on me and smiled. His eyes were crazy, his crazy black mane was wilder than ever. "How am I gonna move this shit? I wanted *money*."

"That's your problem," I choked.

"I'll let you answer differently," he said, eerily calm. He waved his revolver at my stomach.

I kept my mouth shut.

"You know," he began. "I thought you were smarter, Michael Beatrice Evans. I thought you'd be able to figure it out. I thought you'd have the common sense to keep your monkey out of the game. Guess not. Guess you're pretty fuckin' stupid, aren't you? And now you saunter in here, expecting me to take your thirty pieces of silver with a smile? I don't think you understand what's *really* going on here, Michael."

"But we got your money."

"Money?" He smiled and gently pushed me away. "Go. Get the fuck out of here, before I change my mind."

I turned and walked out. I left the silver on the floor behind me. I knew I'd look fuckin' bad in front of the others. I had to look calm. I guess I didn't know what else to do.

I opened the car door and got in. Everyone looked at me.

"You okay, Michael?" Kat asked, concerned.

I paused for a second.

No, I am not okay.

Just say it.

"Yeah, I'm fine," I said. "It went well. He took the silver."

They went back to their celebration.

I sat in my seat, paralyzed.

I'd never been so scared.

What did he want from me?

3

The fax arrived five days later, on Friday.

Logan Canton had been kidnapped.

Here's what happened.

4

I came home Sunday night and sat on my bed, still shell-shocked.

Thomas poked his head in. "All right, Michael! We're all done! We can go back to being normal! In Normal!"

Thomas laughed at his own joke. I laughed, too. But it was forced. "Good one, man. Low effort, but good."

Thomas' smile disappeared. "What's wrong?"

"What makes you say that?"

"You just seem . . . *off.* Shouldn't you be celebrating more? It's finally over! Fuck Mr. Sanders!"

Fuck Mr. Sanders.

The insult hung in the air.

I winced.

"No," I lied to his face. "Nothing's wrong. I'm fine." I forced a smile. "Just a little shaken from doing all this, that's all. Glad it's over."

Oh, if only it had been true.

"Ah." His grin returned. "Well, cool. Just checking in on you."

He left.

I lay back and stared at the ceiling.

5

Monday was a doozy. I wandered the halls at school, dead inside after not getting any sleep.

I was on my way to lunch when I caught the eye of Eric, my aggressive creditor. He put on a Joker grin and beelined toward me. I dropped my stuff and tried to make a run for it, but he was too fast. He clamped his hands around my arms and slammed me against the wall.

"You've got some fucking nerve."

I looked up at him, too scared to struggle.

He wasn't drunk.

I couldn't decide whether that was good or bad.

"Listen, dude. I have your money."

He whispered in my ear. "That's the biggest load of shit I ever heard."

"No, asshole. I have your damn money. I managed to get it."

"Then why isn't in my fucking hands?"

"Ow! Fuck! It's not in your hands because it's not liquid yet!"

He loosened up a bit. "What the hell does that mean?"

For how much he frightened me then, I had to laugh at how stupid he was. "It's not in cash form yet."

He scoffed. "What? You rob a bank or something?"

The color drained from my face.

He laughed out loud. "You're such a weak-ass bitch, Evans." He wiped tears from his eyes. "Oh, that's good. Look, I don't care where you got the money or what it looks like. I just want it. And because I've been waiting so long I'm gonna take triple. Nine hundred bucks. That sound about right?"

I was screaming inside, but I nodded. There was Mr. Sanders to worry about. This guy was chump-change.

He smiled. "Get it to me by Wednesday. We'll meet

at my car, pot-lot, before school." He leaned forward. Our noses were almost touching. "I swear to God, you don't have my money by then, you're gonna spend the rest of your life drinking dinner through a straw."

He let go and walked away.

I slid to the floor, my head in my hands.

6

Tuesday also sucked. I had a chat with my math teacher, Mr. Philips, about my plummeting grades.

"I'm concerned about this." He frowned. "You're not applying yourself."

To tell you the truth, I actually liked him. I thought he was kind. He took the time to learn about everyone. But I was in no state of mind to consider that. "I don't really care about my math grade."

"But you did last semester," Mr. Philips said. "You even cared just a few weeks ago."

"Yeah, well I don't care now," I snapped. "Get off my balls, will you? You're not my dad."

I expected him to get angry. Instead, he looked down at his feet. "It's like you've given up. And not just in math."

I felt like I'd been punched.

He just cared about me.

Just like they all did.

But I was too freaked out.

I stood up. "Don't worry about me, all right? Just leave me alone."

7

Logan wasn't in school for the second day in a row.

"Why's Logan gone again?" I asked the gang at lunch.

Shrugs.

"Beats me," Ryan said. "Must've gotten sick."

"He was fine when we saw him Sunday morning."

Bastard frowned. "I don't know. You can get sick pretty fast."

Kat was looking at her computer. "You're right. He is sick." She looked up. "I just got an email from his mom."

"Since when does his mom write emails?" Ryan asked. "I don't even think she knows how to use a mouse."

"I know it's odd," Kat admitted, "but it's what we've got."

Everyone went back to their food.

I sat there, on the edge of panic.

Even then, I didn't believe his mother's explanation.

Not one bit.

And now I'm here writing this, and I know what happened.

I should've been screaming bloody murder.

But I didn't say a word.

Not one word.

8

Thomas dropped me off at the pot-lot—where all the stoners hung out—on Wednesday at seven o'clock.

I got in Eric's car on the passenger side, carrying a silver bar wrapped in a grocery bag.

"You have it?" He asked.

I nodded and opened the bag. "Here you are," I pulled a bar out. "One 100-ounce bar of silver. Should be worth around fifteen hundred bucks."

I handed it to him.

He stared at it. "This isn't what I asked for."

I flinched. "You said you didn't care how you got it, so I'm giving it to you in silver."

He sighed. "Fine."

"Now, can you stop fucking hazing me?"

"No guarantees. Get out."

He shoved me out of the car and slammed the door. I brushed myself off and walked to school, annoyed.

The rest of the day went okay, I guess.

I spent lunch negotiating with my other creditors over when their money was due. Now that I had assured them that I had the money, most of them agreed to let me get their cash to them when I could. None of them wanted silver and I was glad for that; I still needed to figure out how I was going to turn all that metal into cash.

All the while I talked, though, I was staring at Logan's empty seat.

9

My friends began noticing my behavior Thursday at lunch. I fidgeted in my chair, eating my lunch without an appetite. I was preoccupied, paranoid.

"You okay, Michael?" Thomas asked.

I looked up. Everyone was staring at me. I averted my eyes. "I'm fine."

"Bullshit," Kat said. "You've had bags under your eyes all week, you mutter to yourself in the halls, and you say almost nothing at lunch! We won! We did it! *What's wrong?*"

I huffed, tired of lying. "I told you guys. I'm fine."

"And we're calling bullshit," Ryan said. "Tell us what's wrong. We can help."

I was about to close myself off again, but something at the back of my mind told me to reconsider.

I sighed and looked down at my food. "Come over to my house for dinner tomorrow. I'll tell you then."

"What's for dinner?" Bastard asked.

I rolled my eyes.

The Bastard.

You gotta love him.

"I was thinking spaghetti. Mom's got a killer recipe."

10

Thursday night had me slowly losing my mind.

I wasn't able to sleep; I tossed and turned in bed.

I hoped that Logan would show back up to school with that goofy grin on his face, saying "I'm back, baby! I was dying for a few days there, but I'm *back*!"

Then we'd all pound him on the back and return to a normal life of cracking jokes and having a good time.

But I was starting to believe that that day would never come.

I can tell you this now: It was the first night that I started thinking that my life was over.

11

Friday arrived.

After a third straight night of no sleep, I felt more dead than alive. My hair was a mess, I felt like I was slurring my words, and I couldn't think straight. I even caught myself putting my socks on my hands that morning. You ever do that? Let me tell you, it's a warning sign, buddy. I crawled through the day, my mind consumed with guilt and worry. I kept thinking about Mom, too. The confessional. "You're a child of God," she'd always say. But it felt like I was in hell.

When I got home that afternoon, I started cooking the spaghetti. Thomas had to take over after I kept pouring the water back out of the pot after I'd filled it. I sat on the couch upstairs, unable to do anything but sit, paralyzed.

What was I going to tell my friends?

12

They arrived at six, everybody feeling good.

"Ooh, something smells good in here!" Bastard proclaimed. He looked at Thomas. "I'm assuming Michael didn't make dinner, then?"

"No, sir," Thomas said. "I had to take over. He was just too tired, I guess."

"Evening, sleepy head!" Ryan exclaimed. He gave me a noogie. I tried to smile, then swatted him away.

"Listen," he continued. "It's not a competition. No one's impressed by how many all-nighters you've pulled."

"I'm not pulling anything," I said. My smile disappeared. I felt awful. "I've just been kept up. Kept up by . . . worry."

The mood plummeted.

I sighed, feeling bad that I'd ruined everyone's day.

Or did I know then that I'd ruined everyone's life?

"Come sit down."

They sat. I paused for a second, wondering how to begin.

And the printer whirled.

As if on cue.

An incoming fax.

The last sound I wanted to hear.

I stood up and walked towards the machine, not wanting to know what was in it.

"Who the hell sent you a *fax*?" Kat asked.

"Who do you think?" I answered emotionlessly.

Everyone exchanged worried glances. They joined me, circling around the humming printer. When it finished, I picked up the lone piece of paper.

It was a picture.

Mr. Sanders smiled happily at the camera, his black goat-hair standing on end like a demonic mane.

He was standing over Logan. And Logan looked like hell. He was bruised and battered, arms handcuffed, his mouth muffled, a noose tied loosely around his neck. His frightened eyes pierced through the photo and into my soul. My heart nearly stopped.

"Oh my God," I whispered.

This was the text below:

THIS IS WHAT HAPPENS WHEN YOU DON'T LISTEN. TOO BAD. HE REALLY WAS A GOOD KID.

HE'S GOING TO BE A DEAD KID SOON.

WAITING FOR YOU IN HELL.

HAVE A NICE NIGHT!

"What a monster!" Kat cried. "What a fucking monster!"

"This's what I was worried about," I said. "I thought Logan was in danger. The meeting between Sanders and I didn't go well Sunday. That's when I knew he was out for Logan."

Ryan screamed. Thomas collapsed on the couch, his hands in his face. Kat did the same. Bastard flailed his arms around, knocking shit off the kitchen counter.

I, meanwhile, continued to stare at the paper, tears of regret coming in a rush.

"Fuck me," I whispered.

I wish I could say it a hundred times.

It was all my fault.

Fuck me.

But I needed to act fast.

I had to rescue Logan.

I looked up. "Hey, guys! Shut up!"

No one listened. In fact, things seemed to get louder. My patience ran out, and desperation took over.

"Guys! Shut the fuck up!"

The pandemonium halted.

Everyone looked at me.

"Look," I said. "I'm just as angry and afraid as you are about this—but it's no use freaking the fuck out!" I took a breath. "We need to get a plan together. We don't know what shape he's in now or where he is, but we need to do something, come up with a plan—."

"No," Bastard spat. "Fuck you, Michael. And fuck your *plans*. I want out of this shit."

My anger boiled. "Bastard, I don't give a shit what you think of me, but Logan's life is on the line. We gotta do something."

"Why the hell didn't you tell us about what happened?" Ryan asked. "You kept this to yourself, and now you may have just killed Logan! *You* killed him!"

"You think I don't fuckin' know that?" I said. "Why do you think I haven't been sleeping?"

"Hear that?" Bastard dug in. "Poor little Michael can't get any sleep. While his supposed best friend is ready to get lynched. Want some Nyquil, poor little boy?"

I ignored him.

Besides, what could I say?

He was right.

My friends stared at me.

I said, "Logan is in serious trouble, we don't have

a lot of time, and I can't do this alone. Unless you want to see a fax of his dead body, listen to me."

I waited for any sign of protest.

I got only glares of grief and betrayal.

"Okay," I said. "Here's the plan."

13

"It's going to have to involve something we've never used before," I began. I led them downstairs, pulled back the carpet, and opened the trap door leading down to the bunker. "My dad showed this to me after my mom was admitted to the hospital."

No one said anything, though they were interested. One by one, they descended the ladder. Once they were all down, I joined them.

"Jesus Christ," Ryan exclaimed. "Why the hell does your dad have an army's worth of supplies? Never figured him for a nutjob."

"I don't know." I shrugged and looked around.

Everyone was looking at me, all asking the same wordless question: *Are we doing what we think we're doing?*

The answer was yes.

I gestured to the wall of weapons. "Take your picks. Grab a bulletproof vest and a gun of some kind."

"Are we really gonna do this?" Thomas asked.

I snorted. "What, you think we're just gonna waltz into the KFK and ask for Logan back nicely? Look, I never said we were actually *using* them."

"Then why are we bringing them?" Bastard asked. He was shaking.

"Precautionary measure," I said. "You want to get killed, too?"

"Oh, fuck." Bastard shook his head.

I sighed. "Just get your stuff together. We're rolling in ten minutes."

We geared up, climbed back out of the bunker hatch, then went into my bedroom, where we slid down to the sewers. I was wearing a bulletproof vest, and I'd grabbed a pistol, a Glock. My dad's favorite, I remembered.

If only he could see me now, I remember thinking.

He'd be so proud.

"Be on the lookout," I warned. "He could've anticipated us being down here."

Nervously we walked, watching and listening for anything out of the ordinary. Everything was quiet apart from the rhythmic steps of our shoes.

The peace came to an end as we approached Ku's Fax Klan. Weird noises were bouncing around the sewer's cement walls, echoing all over the place. Bastard was shaking. No one else looked much better.

We got closer.

The random sounds crystallized.

It was screams of anguish.

It was Logan.

Logan was screaming.

We were out of time.

His voice was getting weaker.

"Come on!" I shouted.

We ran, sprinting around the last turn. Logan's

voice was sounding less like a human and more like a croaking frog. We climbed the ladder up to the KFK bathroom—the cover had been conveniently left open for us—and a new sound came.

It was the sound of someone being beaten.

My arms shook. "All right, asshole!" I screamed. "You let our friend go! We'll gun your crazy ass down!"

There was no answer. I broke into a cold sweat. I signaled Bastard to kick the bathroom door down. It shattered off its hinges. I charged forward with my Glock, adrenaline pumping—.

I stopped in my tracks.

At first, it was the kind of shock you feel when you see one of your childhood friends dangling in the air by a cord from his neck.

The kind of shock when you see his head twisted a hundred and eighty degrees.

And then it was a different kind of shock.

The kind of shock where you're staring at a rubber mannequin, sloppily tied up and painted to look vaguely like one of your best friends, a loudspeaker playing a recording near the end of its loop.

The kind of shock where you realize that you've been tricked.

No one was there.

"What the hell?" Bastard asked. "What the hell? Where are they?"

"Long gone," Ryan said grimly.

"Oh, fuck, fuck, fuck!" Bastard continued. "It's all your fucking fault, Michael! None of this would've ever happened if you hadn't bet on that shitty football game!"

Of course, he was right. But I was angrier at him than ever. "Know what, asshole? At least I *try* to save my friends. Least I've got the balls to do that."

"Mighty big of you, considering you're the one who got him fucked in the first place."

It was true, but I didn't care.

I dropped my gun and tackled him. He actually fired a shot—he actually tried to *shoot* me—but he missed, and then I had my hands on his throat.

He gagged, trying to point his gun at me. Kat and Ryan shoved me off him.

"Enough! Enough!" Kat screamed.

"ENOUGH!" Ryan thundered. I stopped. Bastard stopped. We both looked up.

"Guys." Thomas pointed at the floor below the mannequin. "There's a piece of paper."

I got up, walked over, and picked it up.

It was a picture.

A picture.

A picture of Logan Canton's forehead caved in, blood spattered everywhere on the floor behind him.

"This is your fault," a voice came from somewhere.

I dropped the paper.

I don't really remember what happened next.

Maybe I passed out.

I just don't remember.

All I remember is that my best friend was dead.

I was looking at a picture of my mutilated best friend.

Told you before.

Truly horrific shit.

Did you think I was kidding?

Sanders jumped one more time on the corpse's cracked ribs. Better not do it again, the blood would track into his house.

"No matter," he said aloud to himself, cackling like a demon. "I quite like the smell of dead people."

Sanders had already cut up Logan's body—to be sold on Normal's cannibal market, of course. All that was left was his chest and tattered shoes. It was going to have to be disposed of. The real question wasn't how, but where?

Sanders rubbed his chin. Then snapped his fingers. "That's it!" He took out a map of Normal, circled a location. "The cops'll love this!"

He looked behind him at a painting of his dad, David Ku. "How do you like this scene, Father? If you were still alive, you would've beaten me senseless. But no more! How you gonna beat me when you're dead? Have I fallen from grace? Fallen far enough?"

He laughed and reached for his phone, sat down in a chair while it rang.

Slick picked up.

"Hey, Slick! How you doin', buddy?! Listen, remember that time I helped get you outta trouble with those assholes from Seattle a while ago? Remember our little deal? Well, it's payback time. Do me a solid, okay? Bring up your hunting buddies and stay over at my house for a few days. It'll be worth the wait, I promise. All right? All right. Catch you later, man."

Sanders put down the receiver, poured himself a shot, and toed the mangled corpse. "Wonder if anyone'll show up to this asshole's funeral. Poor sacrificial lamb . . . ."

15

"Logan Albert Canton was kind and loving. He found unfailing happiness in places where nobody else could. He was a good student, a great son, and a special friend. It's heartbreaking to see him go so soon. Oh merciful God, may you absolve this wonderful boy of all his sins and ascend him to heaven . . . ."

The minister continued his sermon.

All I could do was stare at the open grave.

It looked like an open mouth.

A mouth into Hell.

16

After the service, my friends and I sat in the grass until only a few close relatives remained. We cried together long after everyone else had gone.

Finally, Thomas spoke up. "So what now?"

"I don't know," I sniffed. "Guys, I'm sorry—."

"Don't." Bastard glared. "Don't 'be sorry.' You've done enough."

I looked at the grass.

"Bastard, it's not his fault," Kat said. "He didn't kill Logan. Mr. Sanders did."

"No, Kat." I shook my head. "He's right."

She was confused. "What?"

I stood up. "I didn't tell you guys about what happened between me and Sanders. I did kill him."

I walked away.

17

I thought that admitting that it was my fault would help me move on—alleviate the stress and guilt.

But it didn't help.

And then—in my desperation to find something that would help, even a tiny bit—I wound up making another huge mistake.

18

The depression set in fast.

"You're depressed," I said to myself.

Ha!

I've always had a gift for understatement.

I was constantly thinking of ways Logan's death could've been prevented. Like, calling the cops, for example.

But that would bring up the gruesome memories, the picture of his bloody corpse.

And that would bring me back to ways I could've stopped it.

Press repeat.

What I really needed was some way to forget about the whole thing, at least for a little while.

I went into my parents' bedroom (my mother hid the booze there out of fear we might find it in the kitchen and become "sinners," ha!), grabbed a stepstool, opened their liquor cabinet, and grabbed a bottle of white wine.

I stepped down, popped the cork, leaned back, and took a giant swig. The shit was horrible! Better swallow it fast!

Which I did.

It left a bitter taste in my mouth. Not wanting to give up, I tried again. That time, the taste was a lot better but still a bit strange.

By the third swig, the wine tasted nice.

My insides buzzed. I felt warm.

I remember thinking that if this was what adults taste every time they drink, I wanna down this stuff all the time.

So I took another gulp, and then another, and then some more.

The wine bottle was empty, and my head felt like it had been shrunk in a dryer. I tried speaking out loud, but I slurred whatever came out of my mouth.

Damn. Out of wine! Better get some more!

I laughed as I struggled to climb back up the stepstool. I slipped once or twice but managed to get a hold of a bottle of tequila. A shot later, and I was giddy-drunk, barely able to speak. My vision gave out every few seconds.

I started laughing and shouting nonsense as I gulped more tequila. "Haha! Okay, Mom! You were right! I *am* a child of God!"

Gulp.

It was getting a little out of hand now; I was at the point where I'd spilled half of my drink on the floor.

Stupid.

Gulp.

Shit, wasn't I standing up just seconds ago? And what's that warm green puddle doing on the floor?

Gulp.

Ugh, my stomach hurts, everything hurts. I feel as if I'm about to burn up.

Maybe I really was in Hell?

Gulp.

Oh, good God, what's that red stuff in the second green puddle? Oh wait—that's my blood.

Holy shit, my intestines are being pulverized.

My vision blurred, my stomach was emptying faster and faster.

Things became hallucinogenic.

My swirling vision became redder and redder.

I started hearing fire. I started smelling smoke. Flames licked the edges of my vision. A bishop stepped into view.

Behind him was a confessional.

The same confessional as the one in my dream a few weeks ago.

The flames crackled.

Over it all, the bishop shouted: "You must confess, Michael, for you have sinned! For you have sinned! For you have sinned! Fallen child!"

The chanting continued, and then I passed out.

Maybe alcohol wasn't the best solution?

19

Hallow walked into his office Saturday afternoon feeling sad and bitter.

He'd just attended a funeral for a young man whose body—what little was left of it, anyway—had been found on northern Flint Avenue, in one of Normal's sketchier neighborhoods. Police had blocked off the area and had struggled to identify the corpse. The deceased had turned out to be Logan Albert Canton, a high school sophomore whom an officer had interrogated a couple months ago. Forensic scientists couldn't identify the perp—there was no trace of extraneous DNA on the body.

For the Normal Police Department, it was a defeat.

For Hallow, it was work to be done.

BRRRING! BRRRRING!

Hallow answered the phone. "NPD. Hallow."

"Hey, David. It's James."

"Good to hear from you, Chief! How's Haiti?"

"Pretty good. A lot of work sometimes. I don't have much call time, though. Gotta talk to you about something."

Hallow raised an eyebrow. "What's up?"

"I heard about Logan. He was a friend of my son's."

Hallow sighed. "Yeah. This week's been shit. Logan was the one I interrogated on the Dilly Bar case a couple months before, at his place. Makes me think something bigger is going on."

"You still think Logan was involved?"

Hallow looked back down at his computer screen, tapped his thumb on the table. "You know the Depository bank heist two weeks ago? Turns out six people were involved in that—same number as the Dilly Bar scam. Something fishy is going on. Might be the same crew."

"Evidence?"

156

"No," Hallow admitted, "but the coincidence is striking."

"Here's my advice." Evans continued. "If you don't have evidence now, don't invest resources in Dilly Bars. You've got a murder on your hands, man. Fuck the ice cream."

20

When I woke up, my throat was drier than Death Valley, and I stunk like a pig. Half-dried bile was caked to my cheeks. I struggled to stand up. A throbbing headache pounded my skull.

"What the hell," I muttered. I was somehow back in my room and naked apart from my underwear.

I turned for the door and nearly shat myself.

Thomas was sitting at my desk, staring at me.

"Holy shit!" I yelped. "Scared the hell out of me! What are you doing here? What time is it?"

"It's 12:30 in the afternoon," Thomas said. He looked pissed. "What the hell are you thinking?"

I shrunk. "Uh . . . what? What did I do?"

He rolled his eyes.

I nodded. "That is, what did I do *now*?"

"You must be real hungover."

I cradled my pounding head. "Jesus."

"You downed a bottle of wine and who knows how much tequila."

He tossed the bottles onto my bed beside me. I shuddered. "That could've killed me."

"No shit," he said curtly. "What the fuck is wrong

157

with you, bro? Your *smell* could kill you, man. And you look like you slept in the gutter. Why, Michael?"

I struggled to answer. "I wanted to forget, man. Upset at what happened to Logan, pissed—the whole state of things."

"So you get loaded? Nice excuse."

"No! Well . . . yeah . . . . What else can you do? I already have a dead friend; I don't want my brother yelling at me for trying to forget for a couple hours—."

"So you're mad at me for wanting to help you? I should let you drink until you die?"

"Thomas, I'm not—."

"Bro, I get that you're sad. I get how guilty you feel over Logan. But that doesn't give you an excuse to kill yourself. Get it? That doesn't give you permission to refuse my help and get mad at me when I do help you."

He turned around and left.

"Thomas, come on!" I shouted after him. "I'm sorry!"

"Go fuck yourself!" He slammed his door shut.

Seriously.

What the fuck was wrong with me?

21

I got up fifteen minutes later to take a shower.

Filth washed off me, ran down the drain.

Really nice, eh?

After getting dressed, I ate breakfast and tramped down to my computer. After starting a group video call, three faces popped up on the screen. Kat, Ryan, and Bastard all looked tired and sad.

I made up I my mind.

I wasn't going to treat them like I'd treated Thomas.

"Hey, guys," I said, trying to smile. "How's the day been?"

Ryan stared at me. "Fine. Just great. Been catching up on my reading."

"Sounds fun," Kat answered. "Spent all morning holed up in my room. There's some stupid family drama happening downstairs."

Thomas noticed my call from the hallway and sat down next to me. "What kind of family drama?" he asked.

Kat rolled her eyes. "My aunt's been over at my house for a month because her house got foreclosed on. My parents got into an argument with her about why she hasn't left yet." She paused to let us hear the screaming. "Fun stuff. So anyway while I was in my room yesterday, I fiddled around with my laptop. Mr. Sanders has been on my mind."

Bastard closed his eyes.

"Sanders" was now a curse word among us.

I was the first to ask. "Are you worried about him, or what?"

"Kind of." Kat sighed. "I decided to try to find some more information about him."

"Huh?" I asked, confused.

"On the KFK website."

"Okay?"

"It says here that his full name is David Alexander Sanders. His original name was David Alexander

Ku. His address is 13 Baker Avenue. It's on the outskirts of town, at the edge of the forest."

"So what's the point of that? What's that get us?"

"Well, nothing.

Gears started turning in my head.

"We could—," I started.

"No," Thomas said.

I looked over at him.

He continued. "I know what you're gonna say. You're gonna tell us to gear up, then walk casually over to Mr. Sanders' house and take him out. I don't even need to ask if it really was your intention, because it was. I can see it in your face. Haven't you learned a fucking thing? Revenge, Michael? Really? What do you think this is?"

"And why not revenge?" I countered. "Why can't revenge be the solution? And it's not 'revenge.' It's *justice*, man. Justice for Logan, and standing here pulling our peckers isn't gonna do shit."

"Michael." He shook his head. "Wake the fuck up."

"I've had it," I said. "We're doing it. We're killing Sanders, and that's—."

PEEEEEEEP!

Thomas and I jerked.

Kat had a whistle in her mouth, and she was waiting to see if she needed to blow it again. "Shut up. Both of you. Get it together."

With Kat looking as if she was threatening to reach through the screen and beat both of us to death, we mumbled slurred apologies.

Kat relaxed. "Now. We have a problem to solve. Mr. Sanders is exposed for the time being. Michael is right on this one; this could be our only chance to be proactive. If we don't, then we might as well admit we lost."

"But we don't need to be 'proactive,'" Thomas protested. "He's made no moves against us."

"He killed Logan," Kat said.

Thomas looked down at the floor.

He had to give her that one.

"Thanks, Kat," I said.

Kat snapped her fingers to hush me. "Michael, we don't trust you. You're different. Something's happened. You've changed. And not for the better. But this *has* to end. We finish Sanders, and then we're done. Got it?"

"Can't we just go to the cops?" Bastard asked.

I shook my head. "We go to the cops, they've got us for felony breaking and entering, among other things. We started this. We should finish it."

"I'm not going to prison for that bastard," Kat said.

Ryan started to say something, then didn't.

"We doing this?" Kat asked.

I opened my mouth, then shut it, and nodded. "Yeah."

Kat looked at me. "We follow you one last time and then we're *done*."

I nodded again.

What else could I do?

Turns out, she was wrong. And I was wrong, too.

But even if I wanted to stop, it was too late.

At least that's how I felt then.

It felt like we were nearing the end of a long, dark tunnel.

I was sure it was almost over.

But along the way I'd lost my friends' trust and faith.

And I'd gotten Logan killed.

And writing this now, I realize something else: I'd lost myself, too.

22

Everyone came over a little later.

"We all understand what we're here for?" I asked. "We only have one job: Kill Mr. Sanders. We're gonna hit his house, catch him by surprise, gun him down, and gone. Clear?"

They nodded, some more willing than others.

Thomas looked pissed. Ryan was fidgety. Bastard was ready to have a nervous breakdown. Kat was reserved, but I could tell she was worried.

"Good," I said. "Let's head to the bunker and strap on."

23

We grabbed weapons, grenades, and bulletproof vests. We looked like a squad of soldiers. Then, like we always did, we walked to my room and climbed down into the sewers.

"We're gonna be walking down here for a while," I said as we started.

Kat looked at me. "You still haven't told us the plan for when we get to his house. I get what we're doing, but *how* are we doing it?"

"Here's my thought," I began. "I did some research on the address. Turns out that Sanders lives in a mansion. Pretty big one. Swimming pool in the back, the whole deal. The nearest sewer cover is a half-mile away from our destination, and the distance between that is covered in forest. So we're either gonna have to walk through the forest or walk around on the road. Once we get to his house, we'll go in through the back. We'll find him, shoot him, and get out."

"That didn't really answer the question," Bastard said. His face was pale.

"I don't have anything else for you," I said. "I haven't exactly been over there a lot."

"No telling with you," he said.

I didn't say anything.

I was honestly surprised that Bastard hadn't spilled the beans to anybody.

Maybe he was keeping on for the money.

Then again, maybe not.

Not much money in murder.

You see how crazy I was?

Maybe Mom was right.

Maybe I was possessed.

But if I was possessed then, what am I now?

24

"End of the line," I muttered.

We'd reached as far as the sewer tunnel could take us.

I climbed up and opened the sewer cover.

"Coast is clear," I said. "Let's head to the surface."

To anyone watching, we looked dangerous, to say

the least. We wore thick vests, had semi-automatics slung on our shoulders, and carried shotguns.

After another fifteen minutes of hiking, a large building came into view. The letters KU were engraved on the front. The words SANDERS MANSION were hastily scrawled below it. The house was cream-colored, with old sloped roof peaks and decorative windows. A neatly-trimmed lawn draped out front, with a mailbox carved to look like a bear. Thick green hedges surrounded the property—the perfect cover for crawling stealthily around the house.

"Holy shit," Thomas exclaimed. "Big house."

Kat shushed him. "Keep your guard up."

We crept around the place, using the hedges for cover. Near the back of the property, a gap in the hedges revealed the backyard. It was more a courtyard than anything, smooth marble pavers everywhere. A carved fountain statue of Sanders himself sat in the center. It looked like it had been carved by a child; his features looked more like an imp than a human. Near the edge of the property, an infinity pool flowed.

"What in the world?" Kat muttered. "What's the point of all this shit?"

"How the hell could he even afford this?" Ryan asked.

"Dude owns a backwater print shop."

"Guys, we don't have time to gawk at the place." I huddled them up. "Just like we talked about: We'll enter the building and set up blockades around the back door so he can't get away."

"God," Thomas groaned.

"What?" I asked. "You wanna turn around when we're in Sanders' backyard?"

"We always could, though," Bastard suggested. He was breathing quickly, almost hyperventilating. "That's always an option."

"It's okay, Jim," Ryan reassured him. "You'll be all right."

"I'm scared. I want to go home," Bastard moaned.

But there was no stopping now—at least that's what I said to myself then.

Another lie.

So we crept to the back door, turned the handle, and stepped inside. Thomas, Kat, and I quickly surveyed the scene before setting up chairs and tables to serve as cover. I peered into the kitchen—and yelped!

Sanders was sitting at the table watching us. His goat-hair looked extra wild. His eyes smoldered.

Kat and Thomas jumped and reached for their weapons. Ryan tried in vain to calm Bastard, who had started shaking.

I stood there, my heart in my throat.

"Freeze—freeze, you fuck!" I finally shouted, racking my shotgun, aiming at him.

Sanders simply smiled and waved his hand. "I wouldn't shoot if I were you. You've got a rifle aimed at your head." He grinned wider. "You all do. I go down, you all die."

My insides churned, waiting for him to make a move.

He whispered. "I have to ask you twice? Drop your fuckin' weapons."

Bastard shuddered behind me.

I dropped my gun.

"Do as he says," I muttered.

Guns clattered to the floor.

Sanders took out a walkie-talkie. "This is Sanders. Snipers, stand down. Over." He put it back in his pocket. "How's it going, guys? Hey, great job finding where I live!" He paused to qualify. "Glad you're not stupid. Not completely, at least." He shrugged. His eyes looked crazy.

"Why'd you kill Logan?" Kat interrupted. "Why the fuck did you do it, you monster?"

"Monster?" Sanders paused. Then he waved his hand dismissively. "Shut up, slut. The men are talking."

She flinched.

Sanders laughed. "Don't like that word? Ha! But to answer your question, I *did* explain why I had to kill him—when we met." Then he turned and stared at me. "But you just don't listen, do you Michael?"

I went pale. He laughed. "I knew you were coming here. That's why I set up the snipers." Two bearded men in camo walked in from his left. "You see these two? They're itching for blood. And they're gonna get it."

"But . . . but *why*? All this? Why?" Bastard cried. "Who dropped you as a kid?"

"I wasn't dropped," Mr. Sanders said. "And how I came to see the truth about the human race is none of your business. All you need to know now is how fuckin' dead you are."

"Shut the fuck up, man," I snarled. "You blackmailed us for money, destroyed our lives, kidnapped one of our friends, and killed him for fun."

I grabbed my shotgun off the floor.

Aimed.

Fired.

BLAM!

Missed.

Chaos ensued.

Bullets flying everywhere, dust and gun smoke billowed. My ears rang. Sanders made a hand motion to his mercenaries then ducked away, walkie-talkie in hand. I heard nothing but the crazy loud bangs of gun fire.

But the fucker had to pay.

I reloaded my shotgun. My eyes burned with dust. I stood and fired at one of the mercs. Missed again. I lingered for a few seconds, trying to find a target.

Ryan pulled me down. "What the hell are you thinking?" he hissed.

"Trying to see where they are!"

"There're too many thugs firing at us to worry about body count!"

"We should all be grateful for that," Bastard said, tears streaking down his face. "How the hell are we surviving?"

"I don't know," Ryan responded grimly. He stood up and emptied his gun into the dust before ducking down again. "You tell me."

"Damn them," Thomas muttered. "Why can't they just die?"

"Just shut up and keep shooting," Kat said back.

Five minutes passed.

It felt like an eternity.

The gun fight fell into a steady rhythm. I'd sit behind cover, reload, and then duck out and shoot before diving back down to repeat the process. Sometimes I'd just raise my gun without exposing myself.

Dust and shrapnel floated in the air. The stacks of furniture looked like trees after a termite infestation. No one had the chance to shoot anything or anywhere without fear of being shot at from what felt like a dozen directions. How many guys were we fighting? It felt like legion. And it was a miracle we were still relatively unscathed.

Our luck was about to run out.

I heard a sudden THUNK.

I turned.

A grenade rolled around carelessly.

"Shit!" I shouted with surprise, grabbed it, and chucked it. It exploded in the middle of the room, and everybody fell back. My ears rang. Splinters showered everywhere, raking my legs.

"Everyone all right?" I asked, coughing.

Kat covered her face. "Yes. Everybody's fine, aside from a few splinters. Jesus," she moaned. "I think I got one in my eye . . . ."

"They don't seem to be firing back." I peered into the thick dust. "You think some of them might've been hurt?"

Zing!

Squelch!

A stray bullet zipped across the top of my shoulder, burning skin and muscle.

". . . Oh fuck," I said. "Ruined my shirt."

I laughed.

And then I screamed.

Ryan wrapped a piece of cloth around my shoulder.

The others continued fighting. The pain washed through my body—but I must've been in shock. It didn't hurt as bad as I thought it would. "God . . .," I panted, "this isn't working. We gotta get out of here! Guys!" I pointed at the back door. "C'mon!"

We all stood and sprinted out the back door, scrambling to avoid fire as we ran across the courtyard. Thomas stopped in his tracks. "Holy shit!" he shouted. He pointed at the hill overlooking the mansion. "That fucker has a *rocket launcher*!"

Puff!

A soft burst of smoke from the tube, the projectile coming straight at us.

"Down!" I yelled.

We all dove to the ground, the rocket crashing into the side of Sanders' home as if God himself had wrought thunder down. I lost my balance and slammed my injured shoulder into the hedge, but Ryan held me up. We all ran out of the courtyard, hauling ass across the pavers. The heat from the burning house warmed our backs.

We continued sprinting to the forest edge.

"My God," Kat breathed. "We blew it up."

"Not 'we,' Ryan countered. "That asshole blew up his own house, not us."

"It never would've blown up if we hadn't been there," I said, feeling the pain in my shoulder return. I looked to my left. Sanders' goons were all lined up on the road, as if waiting for something.

"To the forest," I ordered.

Thomas frowned. "I'm never going to—."

Mr. Sanders stepped calmly out from behind a tree and covered Thomas's mouth. He jammed a pistol against his head. "One wrong move, fuckers, and I'll blow this shitbird's head off. Drop your guns."

We did.

He cracked Thomas across the head. Thomas went down.

"You little angels burned my house down. This is the price for your transgressions."

He aimed at Thomas's leg.

BANG!

Thomas screamed; his shinbone shattered.

Mr. Sanders kept his gun on him, then smiled at him. "Now get up and get out of here. Run away into the forest, Thomas. Bleed out there—that way." He gestured off into the dark.

Thomas looked at me, one final time, his face a mask of pure horror.

Then, he got up, hopped away into the forest, and disappeared.

Mr. Sanders looked back at me. "Now go, Michael. Take your little friends and go. You still don't get it, child." His eyes burned. His black hair was like frazzled wire. He pointed his gun in my face. "We're not done yet. We haven't even started. Leave your brother to the night. Go. Go, *that* way." He pointed into the woods, in the opposite direction Thomas had gone.

They all looked at me—my friends—not knowing what to do.

Sanders grinned.

His face looked like the devil.

Like the devil himself.

And everyone was still looking at me.

"Go," Sanders whispered. "My guys are out there. My little imps. If you look for him, Michael—your friends will be dead, too."

I turned around a left.

They followed.

And as I slunk away, Mr. Sanders whispered: "How many more will you lose, Michael? How many more are you willing to kill?"

I ran. My friends followed me.

I remember crying.

I remember yelling.

I remember them screaming at me until I covered my ears with my hands and ran away from them, back to my house.

25

I cried myself to sleep that night.

And my dreams weren't any reprieve. I dreamt of Logan's brutal massacre, only this time, when I walked into the burning confessional, I found his body hanging from the ceiling. I saw Thomas's leg shatter over and over again. His face looking up at me for help. Help I'd been too scared to give.

26

After a torturous night, I woke up and mindlessly got into the shower, then walked upstairs for some cereal.

I nearly cried on the way up. I'd always been used to my brother around.

Now he was gone and the house felt lonely.

During lunch—and let me tell you, going to school with all this shit going down felt *surreal*—I sat down at my friends' table. It seemed like they'd got as little sleep as I did.

"How was the morning?" I asked them.

"'How was the morning?' You fuckin' kidding me?" Bastard stared at me with two red, sleep-deprived eyes. "Fuck you, man."

"Yeah," I said. "I just saw my brother shot and left for dead in front of me."

"You left him for dead, you son of a bitch," Bastard hissed.

"We all did," Ryan said. His face was pale.

It was so weird.

We were in school like nothing had happened.

But everything had happened. And yet nobody knew. It was like we were living two lives.

"It's my fault," Kat sobbed.

"Huh?" I frowned.

She sniffed. "If I hadn't snooped around looking for his address, Mr. Sanders couldn't have planned everything in advance. He wouldn't have shot Thomas."

"No, Kat, it's not your fault," Ryan said.

"That a joke?" Bastard interrupted. "Of course it's not her fault." He pointed at me. "It's *Michael's* fault. He wanted to go! He thought that it'd be a good idea to stroll through the sewers and go kill someone!"

"Bastard, calm down—." Ryan began.

"No!" he snarled. "Open your fucking eyes!" He

jabbed a finger at me again. "*He's* to blame! If he never made us go on these shitty little 'missions' of his, no one would be dead! Fuckin' Dilly Bars and bullshit."

"Bastard." I closed my eyes. "You never had to be here. You didn't have to come. You just wanted a quick buck off the whole thing. Remember that?"

He slammed his fists down. "I never expected this shit! I thought it'd just be innocent coupon abuse, so please pardon the fuck out of me if I call it like I see it. It was *you*, Michael. Not Kat, not Mr. Sanders, *you*. Look us all in the eye, Michael Beatrice Evans. Explain how your brother's life was worth a fuckin' Super Bowl bet. Why'd you do it? Why? Can you *explain* it? What the fuck were you thinking?"

"I fucked up," I whispered. My face burned. I looked at my cold food in shame. "I wasn't thinking. I was stupid. I fucked up." I repeated quietly.

"Michael," Kat murmured. "You should go."

I stood up and dumped my uneaten food into the trash.

I was living in Hell.

It was my fault.

Bastard was right. Right from the beginning.

I am living in Hell.

27

After school, I walked back home. My binders were filled with homework I wouldn't do. If there was any solace in my terrible day, it was lost in the forest, along with Thomas.

My eyes swelled with tears. He'd probably bled out on the ground somewhere in that place, begging for death. Beetles and bugs would chew on his flesh, until only bones remained. Eventually, even those would break down and scatter to the wind.

I stepped into the house, took off my backpack, and walked downstairs to find the printer churning out an incoming fax.

I tore off the paper:

BRING ME $1 MILLION BY FRIDAY.

OR I KILL YOUR PARENTS WHEN THEY COME BACK.

28

Down in Haiti, James Evans walked through the church doors, totally exhausted. His wife, Abigail, skipped into the building, lighter on her feet than she'd been in years.

"Oh, it's so liberating, James!" she exclaimed. "I feel so alive! I feel so—I don't know, holy! I've never been this close to God!"

He smiled. "I'm just glad to be spending some time with you."

"Oh, James!" She wrapped her arms around him. "I'm sorry I was so hard on Michael—on our entire family. It was a mistake, putting distance between Michael and I, being so hard on him. I'll make it up to him."

James put a finger to her lips. "It's okay now. Michael's fine, and you're better. That's all that matters."

She sniffed. "I know." She let go of him. "I'm gonna go change. Should we call the boys?"

James nodded. "Sounds like a great idea. We haven't heard from them in a while."

"I wonder why?" she said with a sarcastic wink. She walked to the restroom.

James chuckled. Then he looked at his phone, then opened his browser. He'd been trying to stay off the web since he'd arrived, but why not take a quick gander? He opened the website for *The Normal Daily*.

NORMAL CONTINUES TO GRIEVE

THE LOSS OF LOGAN CANTON

Logan Canton, a 16-year-old at Normal High School, was found dead on Flint Avenue a little over a week ago. The city continues its mourning period into Monday morning. His funeral was held Saturday.

James frowned.

Abigail returned. "What's wrong?" she asked.

He looked up at her. "You remember Michael's friend, Logan?"

"Of course."

"He was murdered the week after we left."

"What?!" Her eyes widened. "How did it happen?"

"It says here that his body was found on Flint. They don't have any suspects."

"That's horrible!" she cried. "We should call Michael right now! I'm sure he's devastated."

29

I stared at the fax.

And then my phone rang.

I answered. "Hello?"

"Hey, Michael. How's it going?"

I groaned and fell back on the couch.

It was my parents. "Hey, Dad," I said weakly. "I thought you were in Haiti. You coming back early—?"

My mom said in the background. "No, we haven't left Haiti."

I sighed with relief. "I bet you're having a great time."

"We're so sorry about Logan, Michael."

They knew.

Of course, they knew.

Why wouldn't they?

I began to cry.

"What happened?"

I cried even harder. "I don't know. I don't know." I cried, lying. "They just found him out on the street."

"Shh . . . ." Dad hushed. "It's okay. It's all right."

"It's not all right," I whispered.

I was suddenly struck by the urge to confess, right then and there. To tell them everything.

If only I'd had the guts.

But I went the other way. "Guys, can I just be left alone? It's too hard to talk right now."

"You sure?" Mom asked, concerned.

"Yeah. I need to go. I've got homework. I want to be alone."

I could hear them sigh. "All right, we'll let you go," Dad said. A long pause. "We love you, son."

"Bye, Dad. Bye, Mom. I love you."

I hung up, ashamed.

More lies.

Lies of omission are lies.

I looked down at the fax, again.

Sanders' message remained.

I'd need a million bucks by Friday.

Better call the crew.

Again.

What a fuckin' joke.

30

They handled it well.

If you consider "handling it well" nearly blowing out my speakers with shrieks of rage.

After a few false starts trying to calm them down, I finally shut them up by grabbing an air horn from my desk drawer and holding down the trigger until the air ran out.

I set down the can. "Could you just let me finish?"

No one answered. Ryan looked at the floor. Kat stared at me, scared. Bastard leaned back in his chair, furious.

"All right," I continued. "Guys, you know our lives are at stake here, right? Mr. Sanders will kill us otherwise."

"What do you need from us?" Kat asked.

I smiled. "Well, something involving you, Catherine. I looked at the paper this morning. Apparently, last year's school bond for the elementary school renovation—thirty million dollars—dropped into the NPSD accounts two days ago. Normal Public Schools are flush with cash. I was wondering—."

She interrupted me. "If we could break into the operation, grab the funds?"

I nodded. Kat rolled her eyes to the sky. "God dammit. If things go south—*again*—I'm blaming you." But she smiled at me and for a second, the world was beautiful.

I smiled back. "Thanks. Hook us up to a network, so we can all mess with stuff.

"A network?" Kat laughed. "I love that you don't know what you're asking for. Hold on."

Bastard had been seething through all of this. And then he lost it. "Fuck you, Michael. I'm done. You fucked us all. You're sick. I'm out."

He hung up.

"Okay, we're in," Kat breathed.

31

Three teenagers—Ryan, Kat, and Michael—sat in their rooms, chatting on their computers. Kat had broken into the NPSD accounting office and transferred the money to Sander's business account that she'd looked up. She'd also given them complete administrative access to all school files. After the transfer, they decided to fool around with the district files. After all, Michael reasoned, there was no harm done if they weren't caught. And it seemed unlikely that they would be. Kat's infiltration had been flawless.

For a little over an hour, they spent time altering things on the server; they reduced the payroll of all school board members and administrators, they raised the salaries of all the teachers, and they changed the vendors for school lunch.

Michael was miserable the entire time. Besides, wasn't he old enough to drop out of school.

So, on a whim, he deleted all evidence of his school records just before Kat closed their network. It'd been a perfect hack.

Almost.

The mistake she'd made was small, so small that it wasn't noticed until three hours later by an over-worked NPSD accountant. He contacted his superiors who then brought in cryptologists to find the source of the intrusion.

Michael closed his computer.

He was officially a high school dropout.

He'd sent a million dollars to Mr. Sanders.

Michael had broken into a school server and stolen a million dollars in public funds.

Michael had committed his fourth act of crime.

V

1

Hallow and Charlie walked into work Tuesday morning, ready for the meeting ahead of them. It was their annual appeal to the city council for additional funding, and it was meant to be a serious affair. In reality, however, the NPD knew that no matter how good a case they made to the council, they'd get nothing more than a thank-you-very-much and a firm handshake. As a result, no one took it seriously.

"Morning, ladies and gentlemen," Hallow announced.

Everyone murmured back.

"In five minutes, we're gathering with city council members to discuss our annual budget."

The murmurs were replaced by groans. "I know, I know," Hallow agreed, "But we have to do it. It'll only take an hour; it's not gonna kill anyone. We'll be starting in a few minutes, so get ready for some fun."

Everyone milled about. Hallow leaned over and whispered to Charlie, "I'm gonna talk about the Dairy Queen case at the end."

Charlie frowned. "What the hell? *Why*?"

"You'll see." Hallow poured himself a cup of coffee before heading into the council chambers. "Besides, what's the worst that could happen?"

At the head of the conference room, Hallow turned to face everyone, then nodded to the city council.

"All right, everyone, take a seat. Take a seat."

It took a moment for everyone to find chairs. Once they were settled, Hallow began.

"Good morning, council members. We're all here today to discuss matters of security and safety here in the city, specifically what it costs."

He turned on the projector.

"Council, the department understands that Normal isn't in its glory days anymore. Our roads are falling apart, our sewers are infested, and our historic monuments have seen better days. The department works day and night to clean up the worst of the scum, but what we really need right now to get the city back on its feet is more funding. Matt, take it away."

Matt Fink cleared his throat and clicked the projector. "Thanks, Hallow," he said. "Council, our latest violent, theft, and class-based crimes have gotten worse. The number of homicides per 100,000 people has jumped from twelve to twenty-one in the span of only a year." He pointed at a chart. "Of these twenty-one murders, twelve of them were on Flint Avenue and surrounding neighborhoods. One of these murders was particularly nasty, involving a 16-year-old named Logan Canton just weeks ago."

The room went quiet. Matt took a moment before flipping to the next slide. It was a picture of the Normal County Depository after the robbery. "Now, the number of burglaries and thefts in Normal has also increased. When it was robbed, the Normal County Depository lost an estimated $180,000 in silver. With escalating crime of this sort, more money is needed to keep Normal safe. If funding is increased by a modest ten percent, those resources will be put to much needed use. Charlie?"

Charlie nodded and stood. Matt took a seat.

Charlie hated PowerPoint; he simply wrote down some notes for his part.

He coughed. "I'll be brief with this."

He picked up a dry erase marker and drew on a nearby whiteboard. He wrote out the number "1,000" before setting down the pen. "An estimated thousand-plus people are brought here via human trafficking annually. Normal serves as a stop between the larger Canadian and American 'markets.' In addition, around half a ton of drugs are brought into Normal's city limits every year. We're currently dealing with the most monumental narcotic ring in Idaho. We need more funding, now more than ever. Thank you."

Charlie sat.

Hallow stood. "I'd like to address one more issue pressing Normal." He looked over at Charlie, who gave him a frown and thumbs-down. Hallow looked at the council members and continued. "It's . . . an odd case, to be sure."

He picked up Charlie's marker and turned to wipe down the whiteboard. He then drew four crude drawings: a Dilly Bar, a dollar bill, a body, and a burning house. He wrote the number "6" below the Dilly Bar. "In mid-February, six people in assorted costumes started queuing up for Dilly Bars using illegally printed coupons. Around the same time— three days prior to that, in fact—Logan Canton's house burned to the ground. A little over two months later, a massive heist occurred in the Depository. In both cases, six people were involved. The Friday after, Logan's body was found on Flint Avenue."

He let the information sink in. "This is the Dilly Bar

case. One working hypothesis is that Logan Canton wanted to help his family after his house burned down. This led him to robbing the Depository and to the Dilly Bar scam. Since the bank heist, positive public opinion of Normal citizen safety has dropped from sixty to forty percent. The perpetrators of these crimes have had an impact on the public perception of Normal. I know this case is strange, but it's a perfect example of the kind of unusual crime that we're facing these days. We need funding to solve cases like these. With additional funding, we could bring on a few more guys, solve big cases, and improve public opinion—."

"This is a little odd," the council chair interrupted. "You're using *Dilly Bar* fraud as an argument for annual departmental funding?"

"It's just an interesting example. All these crimes are serious in their own right." Hallow nodded. "I do happen to think it's one crew, but that doesn't have anything to do with the budget."

"Maybe." The chair inclined his head. "But I'm worried that you're—."

Right at that moment, as if on cue, an officer came rushing in with a letter in his hand. She ran to Hallow, handed it over.

Hallow opened the letter.

It was from the Normal Public School District.

He scanned it.

Electronic theft.

Yesterday afternoon.

A million dollars had just been stolen.

Hallow couldn't help it.

The first place his head went: the Dilly Bar Gang.

2

Mr. Sanders walked out of Ku's Fax Klan, giddy with delight. He carried a gallon of gasoline and a box of matches. His wiry black hair stuck out in all directions.

It was 3:30 AM.

"Showtime!" he cackled as he stuffed the materials into the back of his pick-up. He backed out, knocked over a trash can, left the lot of the KFK, and got on the road. The small photo of his dad that he kept taped to the dash stared at him as he drove down the street.

"Who are you looking at, Dad?" he asked. "What? Wanna know why I've got all this shit in my bed?" He chuckled. "Starting a fire, of course! Little Hell on Earth! Fucker blew up our mansion, Dad. Four generations of the Ku family, including you. Now it's a pile of rubble. They knock-knock-knocked on Heaven's door." He shrugged. "Time to turn up the heat."

Sanders pulled into Michael's driveway, got out of the truck, opened the gas can, and poured it on the side of the house. Not a lot—just enough to catch the little angel's attention, freak him out a little. He struck a match, tossed it against the house, and the wall erupted into flames.

Sanders walked to his car and slipped into the driver's seat. He grinned, watched the little fire eat away at the house for a second, then sped away.

The deed was done.

He'd always had a penchant for fire.

3

I woke up to the smell of smoke.

"What the fuck?!" I yelled, springing up and grabbing my phone. I couldn't see any smoke. But I could most definitely smell it. I ran upstairs.

And I could hear fire, too. It was outside.

I dialed 9-1-1.

"9-1-1. What's your emergency?"

"My house is on fire. I need help!"

"What's your address, sir?" the lady asked. "Is there anybody in the house besides you? Where are you right now, sir?"

"100 Rivertown Road—right down the road from the South Fire Station. I'm the only one here."

"Sir, you need to get out of the house. The firemen will be there as soon as they can."

"Thanks," I shouted and hung up. I grabbed our fire extinguisher and ran out onto my front porch. The sun wasn't up yet. The side of my house was on fire, the whole wall to the roof, black smoke billowing. I could already hear the fire trucks down the block. I sprayed the fire with my extinguisher, but it didn't do much. And then the fire trucks arrived and were shooting jets of water at the side of my house. Within minutes, the outside fire had died down to a hissing smoke. Two firemen ran inside.

A fireman approached me. "If it's any consolation, looks like it only got this side and a part of the roof there."

"Thanks."

"Don't mention it." The two firemen came back and spoke with him. "Looks like it's still safe to live in, only this side wall and window are bad. No structural damage. Inspector's gonna have to come look at it, too. We're also going to try and determine the cause of the fire. Seen this kind of thing before. Doesn't look like an accident."

I turned around and walked inside, the anger building in my chest again.

Sanders.

It was him.

Definitely.

He'd tried to burn down my house.

And why wouldn't he?

"After all," I said to myself, "he thinks you blew up his house."

And then I stopped short.

"Doesn't look like an accident."

I remembered the note I'd seen in the KFK during that first visit. Something about "Amanda." Could it be that she had something to do with Sanders? Could he have been the one to burn Logan's house down, too?

I was too tired to think about it.

Just needed a little cat nap.

I had a feeling it was gonna be a big day.

I wasn't wrong.

4

I woke up three hours later to the sound of the newspaper hitting my front door window, hard. Exhausted, I rolled out of bed and walked to the front door, mostly out of habit.

I grabbed the paper and sat down on the stairs. I slipped the plastic bag off the roll and began reading:

TEEN FOOTBALL QB COMMITS SUICIDE

Sophomore Jim Ulrin, for unknown reasons, hung himself in his bedroom Monday night. Police are . . . .

I stopped reading.
Bastard was dead.
"Oh, no." I groaned. "Jim, no."
I needed to stop.
It needed to stop.
And I would stop it.

5

Mr. Sanders drove back to Ku's Fax Klan and got a fine night of sleep. At 7:00 AM, he woke up refreshed. After a quick swig of beer, he started reading the morning paper. The front page headlined Jim Ulrin's suicide the previous night.

Sanders chuckled. "Knew he wouldn't last long, little whiner." He looked up at David Ku's portrait hanging above the desk. "Isn't that right, Dad? Don't you agree? You're all-knowing, aren't you? Bet you knew the fuckin' pussy would crack like an egg."

He opened a second beer. "Three down, three to go. Logan had been by far the hardest, but the most satisfying. Thomas had been great, too. And I didn't even have to do anything with Bastard!"

He rocked in his chair. "These next three will be tricky. Kat will be the easiest, dumb bitch. With Ryan, I can just climb through his window in the middle of the night, do him there. As for Michael— well, I like the idea of torture until suicide. Run him through the nine circles of Hell!"

His dad's portrait stared back at him.

"Just remember, Father, it was all because of you and Amanda. If you hadn't introduced us, if she hadn't cheated on me, none of this would've happened. Just remember that." He smiled and took another sip of beer, raised his glass at the portrait.

Time to get back to work on Michael. He'd only used enough gas to scare the kid. Now it was time to *really* turn up the heat.

He stood up, preparing to flip the store sign from CLOSED to OPEN.

"Dad, I'm going to fax him again. He's going to pay me another million dollars for the fire that he stopped. Then, when he's all done with that, I can slaughter the three of them." He chuckled. "Oh, if only this could go on forever."

He cleared his throat and flipped the door sign.

"Open for business!"

6

I got another fax at about nine in the morning.

Mr. Sanders wanted another million dollars in five days.

I wanted to be mad.

But I couldn't manage it.

I was just scared.

He was gonna kill me.

I knew it.

"No." I shook my head. "I will live."

I hung my head.

"But how . . . ?"

But I already knew.

I had to kill Sanders.

Not with a gun.

I needed something bigger.

I needed a bomb.

7

After sketching the blueprints from something I found online, I started a call with Kat and Ryan.

They were both in tears.

"Jim's dead!" Ryan sobbed. "He killed himself!"

"Ryan, you had nothing to do with it. It's not your fault." I didn't know what else to say.

"Never said it was my fault, Michael!" He wiped the tears from his eyes. "He was my friend, and he killed himself. Can't I be sad about that?"

"Hey, hey, Ryan, calm down," Kat sniffed.

"No!" Ryan shouted. He put his face on his knees and began to rock. "I can't! I just want my friend back!" He glared at me. "Why the hell aren't *you* crying, Michael?"

"What?" I asked. "I've cried too much already."

"Bullshit, man. You're getting off on this. The only explanation."

"Guys, stop this," Kat said.

"What're you talking about, Ryan?" My mouth moved on its own, without thought. "What makes you think I even *liked* the Bastard, anyway?"

"See? See?! There's the proof!"

"He's just another person that died. People die all the time. To me, he was just another person."

Yes, I said that.

I don't know why.

But it's true.

Ryan stared at me with disbelief. "He was your *friend*, man! And you're the reason he killed himself!"

Kat started. "Michael, Ryan, stop this—."

"No, Kat!" Ryan exploded. "We're not stopping this!" He stopped short, took a breath, and leaned his head against his chair. He sighed.

"What did you call us for, Michael?" Kat asked.

They stared at me.

I sighed.

I just couldn't escape.

"Guys, Sanders wants another million dollars in five days."

Ryan and Kat's faces were blank.

After a long moment, Kat said, "I should have expected as much."

"How we gonna get the money?" Ryan asked, monotone. He looked exhausted.

"Well," I said, "we're not going to get any more money. It's too dangerous and reckless. We've learned our lesson."

Kat scratched her head. Ryan looked confused.

"What are you gonna do then?" he asked.

"Attack him again," I said.

They groaned.

"I'm out." Ryan shook his head. "Not doing it. You're on your own."

"You're right." I nodded. "I'm going to do it myself. A bomb."

"You can't be serious," Kat whispered.

"I am serious."

And I was.

Ryan shook his head. "Are you fuckin' *crazy*? A bomb. Like a terrorist?"

"Ryan, you don't understand. You haven't heard my whole story yet—."

"I don't need to!" Ryan stared at me. "I've heard enough! I don't want to be the next Oklahoma City bomber! And what if it *doesn't* work, dude? Ever think about that? Sanders will hunt you down. He'll hunt *us* down."

"And what if the bomb works?" I countered, lamely. "Problem solved."

"Ha!" Ryan barked. "'Problem solved,' he says. Yeah. If the bomb goes off, idiot, you'll be tracked down by the FBI, you'll be in jail for the rest of your life." He shook his head, suddenly strangely calm. "I've had enough. Michael, I never want to see you again. You talk about planting bombs and killing people and act like you're just going for a Sunday drive. We're done."

He hung up.

I was shaking.

I'd lost a friend.

Another friend.

Kat watched me. "Michael, he's not just upset

with you. He got mad at me earlier—something I told him."

I looked at her. "And what was that?"

She smiled sadly. She looked so beautiful. "I'm moving, Michael."

"What?"

"We're moving back to Boise. My father was promoted at his firm. And all this. . . ." She waved around. "It's just too much."

"What? But . . . No!" I protested. "You're leaving, too?"

"Goodbye, Michael."

Kat's face disappeared, leaving me to stare at my own dim reflection.

8

I built the bomb that night.

And then I got screaming drunk.

Drank until I couldn't stand up.

Drank until the bishop started screaming in my head.

"You must confess, Michael, for you have sinned. Fallen child of God! You must confess, Michael, for you have sinned! YOU MUST CONFESS, MICHAEL, FOR YOU HAVE SINNED!"

It was the beginning of the end.

I knew it.

9

Early the next morning, Thomas limped to the front door of his house, opened it, and slipped inside. Closing the door behind him, he stared at the state of the place.

"Oh man." He shook his head—and recoiled in pain. Even the smallest gesture hurt. He leaned down, looked at the wound on his leg. It was covered with a makeshift bandage, swollen with blood and puss.

Thomas limped upstairs for some food. The fridge was empty except for some sandwich fixings. He took everything out and started making one. He'd barely finished making it when he glanced over at the counter and saw the bomb.

He took a closer look.

Crude. Homemade.

But it was a bomb, all right.

"What the hell, Michael?" he whispered, looking around the place.

An empty wine bottle sat on the kitchen table.

Thomas walked through the living room, smelled booze, and made his way to his parents' bedroom. There he found his brother sprawled out on the floor, his head resting in a pool of vomit.

Thomas winced and got down on his knees. "Why?"

Michael didn't respond.

Rage swelled in his mind, but he quelled it. "I still love you, Michael. I don't want to leave you like this."

He went back into the kitchen and looked at the

bomb. Thomas choked up. "Jesus. No matter what you did, I still love you."

From the bedroom, Michael murmured in his drunken state.

Thomas started cleaning him up. He took a warm cloth and wiped his little brother's face and hands, took off his stained shirt, and covered him with a fresh, white sheet. When he was done, he looked at Michael for a long time.

"I'm leaving, Michael. I'm leaving Normal for good. Starting over. I turn eighteen in a couple weeks. I'll be able to get a license and a house. I can't stand it here—I don't know how all this happened. It seems like it started so innocently. Stealing some Dilly Bars, man." He cleared his throat. "Goodbye, Michael."

He packed some things and left, stepping out into the foggy night.

Michael slept on in a drunken stupor.

Like nothing had happened.

10

Hallow walked into the station the next morning, ready to work.

"Charlie!" he called out. "Meet me in my office!"

Just as Hallow sat down at his desk, Charlie walked in. "You called?"

"Yeah." Hallow nodded. "You get access to the NPSD network?"

"Yep. Didn't take long after you left. Site access in your inbox."

"Super. You're gonna be with me for the day. Get your laptop."

"All right," Charlie shrugged, fetched his computer, and sat down. Hallow typed in his password. The inbox loaded, and a dozen unread emails flashed before him. He clicked on the one from Normal Public Schools, then clicked on the link and typed in the administrative username and password they'd been provided.

"What do you think we're going to find in there, Chief?" Charlie asked.

"Gimme a minute," Hallow muttered as he looked closely at the website. "I hope to Christ they didn't just immediately revert anything the hacker changed."

Charlie shook his head. "Nope. They didn't. In fact, they kept both copies of the site, before and after the hack. Here, I'll show you."

Hallow pushed the keyboard over, and Charlie typed for a moment. Two windows popped up. One window showed the website before the attack. The other window showed the website immediately following it. David studied the two windows for a few minutes, looking for anything different between the two.

"Looks to me like, with the exception of the million dollars and the superintendent's payroll, all changes occurred on the Normal High School website." He paused. "Charlie, crack your laptop and tell me every case we've had in the high school."

Charlie opened his computer and pulled up the case files.

Hallow's mind raced.

He kept looking at the two NPSD websites, clicking through to enrollment. There was a change there. The number of people attending the high school was different between the two.

He looked up who was missing.

Michael Beatrice Evans.

Hallow leaned back in his chair. "Holy shit."

Charlie turned his laptop around, showed Hallow his screen. "There haven't been any cases at NHS in over a year, Hallow. Pretty much crime-free."

"We've got something better." He tapped his monitor. "Just three days ago, the number of 'Michaels' in the school was eleven. Now, there's ten. The file that's been removed is of one 'Michael Beatrice Evans.'"

"Whoa." Charlie breathed.

Hallow looked at him. "Yeah. You got that right. The Chief's son."

"His house burned, too. Fire says it's arson, for sure."

"Just like the Canton residence. Just before Logan Canton was killed." He stood up. "I'm going to go talk to him."

"Won't he be in school?" Charlie cocked his head. Hallow waved the question aside.

"He deleted himself. I don't think he's there. I think he erased his files, trying to avoid his parents being involved in the process. Doesn't understand how computers work." Hallow chuckled. "It's ironic. His attempt to erase evidence created evidence."

Charlie nodded. "You want me to get an arrest warrant?"

"Not yet."

"Why?"

"Because we don't know what's really going on." Hallow smiled and grabbed his keys. "See you soon, Charlie."

"Good luck."

11

I fluttered awake. A huge headache pounded. My body was unwilling to get up on its own.

"Ugh," I muttered to nobody. "Five more minutes."

Then I remembered what'd been happening, I jumped up, expecting to walk through vomit. But there was nothing. And I wasn't that dirty, either. That much was a relief. I fumbled for my phone, turned it on, eyes wide. It was nine in the morning, almost twenty-four hours later.

"How much did I drink?!" I asked myself, bewildered.

I stood, walked to the bathroom, and looked in the mirror. At least I didn't drink as much as my first time; I didn't quite have as much of that "hangover look." My breath smelled, though. I brushed my teeth, slipped on a new set of clothes, checked on my bomb—.

KNOCK. KNOCK. KNOCK.

"NPD. Need to ask you a few questions, Mr. Evans."

I froze.

KNOCK. KNOCK.

"I can see you through the glass, Mr. Evans. Open up."

I swallowed. "Be right there, officer."

Quickly and quietly, I put the bomb in the oven. Then I splashed some more water on my face and sauntered over to the front door and opened it.

A lone police officer.

"Hi. I'm Officer Hallow, NPD. Are you Michael Beatrice Evans?"

I nodded. "What's wrong, officer?" Tried to play it cool.

He took out a piece of paper and handed it to me. There was a list written on it:

- Dilly Bar coupons
- depository heist
- Logan C.'s murder
- Jim U.s suicide
- hack on the NPSD computers

Yep.

He knew.

Hallow studied me, took some notes. "So. These cases." He pointed to the paper. "Know anything about them?"

I slowly nodded. "Yes. They're crimes I read about in the paper. I know all the guys, obviously."

"So you did know Logan and Jim?"

"You know I do."

Hallow took more notes. "The criminal cases . . . . You think the same crew could've done them all?"

"Why're you asking me?" He didn't answer. I shook

my head and shrugged. "Don't see why not. Then again, it's a bit of a stretch. I honestly don't know."

"Any specific reason why you dropped out of high school now? Funny how that happened the same day as the NPSD hack, isn't it?"

Of course, the NPD managed to get into the NPSD system.

It was the first time I realized that I might not only be a criminal. I might be an idiot, too.

So I lied.

"School just doesn't help for what I'm planning to go into: entrepreneurship. As for the hack, well, didn't even know the school had been hacked. Just a coincidence, I guess."

He finished writing.

And then he smiled at me.

His smile looked fake as fuck, and I bet he knew it, too.

"That's all I needed, Mr. Evans. Thanks for the time. Have a nice day."

And just like that, he turned around and walked to his squad car.

I shut the door, locked it, put my face in my hands.

He knew.

There's no way he didn't.

I was a prime suspect.

My answers were all he needed to get a warrant to take me away.

I looked back toward the kitchen, to the oven, to the bomb inside.

I had to blow up the KFK and get the hell out of Normal.

I needed to end this—to end Sanders—once and for all.

12

So I took out my phone.

I wanted to call my parents.

In a few weeks, they'd be back to find two of my friends dead, Thomas dead, and me in prison for masterminding crimes involving theft, fraud, and murder. My parents deserved to know what had happened, why I did what I did—if I could even explain it. Although now that I'm writing this, I don't think I could have. Either way, I needed to talk to them one last time.

I dialed my mother's number, sat at the foot of the stair, and waited for them to answer.

"Hi, you've reached the voicemail of Lay Minister Abigail, head of St. Francis Ministry in Normal, Idaho. I'm sorry I can't get to you. If you'd like to call back, I can be reached at . . . ."

"No!" I shouted. "Pick up the phone!"

I called again. No answer. I called my dad. No answer. I scowled and hung up.

This couldn't wait.

I entered my mom's number again and waited until the message tone sounded.

"Hey, Mom. It's Michael." I tried to smile, but it felt hollow. "I need to tell you something." I stopped. It was the confession she'd always wanted. "I want to take you back to February. After finals, the Super Bowl was gearing up, so I bet on the game. Against the Patriots. But they won. I owed $20,000, so I decided to start up a Dilly Bar scheme to make the money, but that led to me meeting a maniac from Hell who I owe more money to and all kinds of crazy stuff. Now Thomas is gone, Logan's been murdered, and Bastard committed suicide." The tears started; I felt like I was going crazy. "I'm gonna take a bomb and blow up the guy—and myself, too, I guess. All my friends are gone. And it's all my fault. It's all my fucking fault." I wiped my face. "I'm sorry—."

KNOCK. KNOCK. KNOCK.

"Open up, Michael Evans! You're under arrest!"

"Right on time," I said to the door. I turned back to the phone. "I love you, Mom. I always have. I love you, Dad." I picked up the bomb. "Goodbye."

"Open up, Michael. This doesn't have to get any worse."

I shut my phone, slipped my bomb into my backpack, and crept down into the basement.

From a distance, so far away: "Open up, Michael! It's not too late."

But it was.

At least that's what I thought then.

I slid open the sewer cover in my room.

Above me came a splintered crash, the front door busted down.

I slipped the cover back into place above me, then I hoisted my backpack and its deadly contents over my shoulder.

I wasn't scared any more.

I wasn't mad.

I felt strangely at peace.

Maybe I was possessed, just like Mom thought.

Maybe I am possessed.

I don't know.

But I do know that this is almost over.

13

About half an hour later, I arrived at the sewer exit for the KFK.

I popped the cover and crawled out. Nobody was around. I snuck over to the side of the store, broke one of the basement windows, unlatched it, slipped down inside. There, I took the bomb out of my backpack and armed it, keeping the safety firmly locked down over the detonator. Then I crawled back out the window.

A voice came from behind me: "Right on time, Michael."

I looked up.

Sanders, of course.

Standing there, calm.

He didn't have a gun.

I stood up, looked him in the eye, and lifted the detonator so he could see it.

He grinned. "Good. You're doing so well. You're almost there."

He took a step toward me.

I held up the detonator. "Take another step, fucker, I press this button and boom—low-budget fireworks show. We both go with it, straight to Hell."

He stopped. And his smile widened. His black hair was wild. Teeth super white.

But for once, it felt like I had the upper hand. "You

didn't think I'd do this, did you? Thought I was too much of a chicken, eh? You fuckin' monster?"

He started clapping, slowly. "Good job. But you're wrong about one thing. I knew you'd do this. Knew it all along. It's a damn good plan, Michael. Almost as good as I would do. Your *pièce de résistance.*" He made a kissing gesture, then winked. "Though, if you think about it for a second, if you use a bomb, aren't *you* the monster?"

"No." I shook my head. "*You're* the monster! You ruined my life! You killed my friends. My brother . . . ."

Mr. Sanders held his hands up. "Whatever you say, Michael. I kill them, you kill me. You're right. We're *so* much different. Hey, could I—?"

He made a clumsy grab for the remote.

But looking back now, I don't think he was even really trying.

I hopped back. "No, asshole."

He smiled. "I thought you said, 'one more step.' But I stepped, and we're both still here. Hm. What do you make of that, eh? All talk, no action? Or are you gonna show me how strong and powerful you *really* are?"

"You're gonna tell me something." I cleared my throat. "That, that note—that note I saw at the beginning of our Dilly Bar nabbing. It said 'Amanda' on it. Explain it. Now."

He laughed. "Oh, Michael. Amanda is Logan's mother. But that's not important. What's important is you and me."

"Bullshit. Logan never said anything about this."

He shook his head. "I never said anything about

Logan knowing or not knowing. But *Amanda* does."
He laughed. "She knows what she did." Mr. Sanders
took a step forward. I took one back. "She's a
cheating whore. But I'm not mad at her. She led me
to you. Father put her in my path for a reason."

I froze. "You were with Amanda?"

"Of course." Sanders grinned, taking another step
forward. "I would've been happy, if she hadn't slept
with that black piece of shit. That's how Logan was
conceived. A 'divine conception.'" He chuckled. "You
see, Michael, I've been pulling the strings the entire
time. I originally was on a mission of vengeance.
I wanted revenge on Amanda. But that mission
led me to you. Now I'm on a mission of mercy. And
mercy demands the truth." He pointed at me. "You.
You're my greatest work. My greatest achievement.
A child of God corrupted beyond repair. Not that it
was hard to manipulate you. All you idiots—so easy
to play. So wrapped up in your own little fantasy
worlds. I'm your puppet master, boy. I *made* you."

I panted. My arms shook. My shoulder seemed to
hurt more than ever.

What did he mean?

What did he want?

I shook my head. "You monster! You . . . You *freak*!"

He smiled. "Ever get the feeling that you're stuck
on 'repeat,' Michael? Like you're talking into a
mirror? *You* made this happen, boy. *You* set me free.
All this." He waved around us. "You're here, ready to
burn it all down. To kill and maim and destroy. And
you call me 'monster.'" His smile was cold. His black
mane seemed to rise like a shock of black goat hair.

"You came to kill, so kill, boy. Do what you're told. Do what you 'have' to do."

He took another step.

He was within tackling distance.

I blinked and leapt away from the building.

Then he smiled, made like he was going to jump at me.

I dodged away, jumped, then ran as fast as I could.

I didn't even look back to see if he followed.

I just pressed the button.

SHOOM!

My eardrums popped. The shockwave shoved me tumbling to the concrete. The stink of smoke and fire. Dust everywhere, my tongue was coated with it. I wobbled to my feet. Fell. The world spun. Something felt broken inside my head. Did I black out for a second? Must have. I stood up, collapsed again, then stumbled around for a few more seconds before crawling into a nearby dumpster and passed out.

Not my brightest moment.

But I'd done it.

I'd really done it.

I'd killed Sanders.

I'd purged the world of his evil.

You see my mistake, don't you?

14

The resulting explosion from Michael's bomb was larger than he'd anticipated. (This should shock nobody, since he knew nothing about making bombs

208

in the first place.) The explosion destroyed the KFK, blew out several adjacent buildings, and killed six innocent customers inside them. A mother and her two boys, walking nearby, were also injured, as were many others. The shock wave damaged surrounding buildings and vehicles in a two-block radius.

Michael had detonated an explosive device.

Michael was responsible for millions of dollars in property damage.

Michael had killed six innocent people.

Michael had committed his fifth act of crime.

VI

1

The sirens woke me. Not the collapsing buildings, not the screams of pain.

The sirens.

When I opened my eyes, I received eyes full of dust and promptly coughed until they watered. I sat up, dug the rubble out of the way, hoping for some fresh air before I suffocated. The mess inside the dumpster was about as bad as what was outside. I reeled and coughed some more and finally climbed out. I stopped for a moment, panting, using my shirt as a filter. After a couple seconds, I opened my eyes again.

Onto a nightmare landscape.

What wasn't blocked by foggy, industrial dust was ruined. Gray powder danced in the air. Fires raged in surrounding buildings.

It looked like a warzone.

What happened?

Stupid question.

I had happened.

But I didn't have time to think about it further.

A voice from behind me: "Hey, fellas! I found somebody over here, by the dumpster! You hurt, kid?"

A shadow appeared out of nowhere and grabbed me by the shirt. It was a cop wearing a gas mask.

I tried to wriggle free.

"I've got him!" he shouted. "He looks OK!" Then he took a good look at me. "I've got him—! Wait a minute. You're Michael Evans."

"Let me go, bastard!" I yelled.

I wrenched myself free and sprinted out of the square.

"Stop!" He tried to run after me. "You're under arrest, boy! You're under arrest!"

I kept running.

Oh, shit.

Right in front of me, a group of officers stood on the other side of the road—almost like they were waiting for my arrival.

Their faces were dead serious. One called out, "Michael, you stop right there!"

I dodged down an alley and hauled ass.

They followed, hot on me heels.

I ran on the road, desperately searching for any car with keys still in it. My legs started to feel like lead.

The cops were coming.

I kept running

They were getting closer.

I kept running.

Bingo!

A red car with keys in the cupholder. I swooped inside and shut the door, locking it.

My hands shook as I turned the ignition.

The engine roared up with a satisfying purr.

The cops were almost on top of me.

Sweating, I shifted gears and punched it, squealed the wheels. Kicking up dust, I blasted out of there in my getaway car.

2

Michael Beatrice Evans drove away from the scene

of his crime. Six people had died in the initial explosion, and another two more had perished from suffocation or from the ensuing fires. It was the deadliest crime in Idaho since the Ruby Ridge standoff twenty-four years prior.

Normal Police followed him in hot pursuit.

Blockades were erected, boxing him in.

After several twists and turns, he abandoned his car and ran into the back alleys, hiding as he made his way home.

There, he grabbed food, water, and cooking supplies, and brought it all down to the basement bunker. He also grabbed a bucket for bathroom business and his laptop.

He climbed down into the bunker, adjusted the rug to fall over the hatch, and locked himself in.

In his house above, he could already hear the cops looking for him.

Michael had stolen a car.

Michael had committed his sixth act of crime.

VII

1

So yeah.

That's it.

That's my story.

No.

I'm serious.

That's how I got here.

It all happened, just like that.

Sure, that last "act" was short. But I wanted this to sound cool—and "The Seven Acts" sounds way better than "The Six Acts," doesn't it? I won't write the seventh, of course. That'll be written for me.

I'd like to say a few things before I go.

It's been two weeks since I crawled down here. It's been rough. I've been eating five feet away from where I shit, and shitting five feet away from where I eat. I've been digging a tunnel, but I'm running out of food. It's almost over.

Wonderful life, right?

Don't forget though, after first semester this year, I actually thought it *was* a wonderful life. When my report card came in with straight As, we went out to eat, and I was rewarded for my hard work by way of the honor roll and proud parents. I was finally starting to think I was going somewhere. I felt on top of the world.

And then the Super Bowl rolled around and I was determined to test my luck and my intelligence—and I fucked up.

And now I'm part of a distinguished club of jack-off murderers, just waiting to be caught and sent to jail.

So far, they haven't found me.

But they will.

Maybe you don't care about this.

Maybe you don't give a shit about me.

You've got every right to feel that way.

I'm not writing this because I'm trying to be relatable or because I want you to sympathize with me.

No.

I'm writing because I'm sorry.

Kat, I'm sorry. I'm sorry I used your genius. I'm sorry I never asked you out on a date.

Ryan and Bastard, I'm sorry I took advantage of you and betrayed your trust.

Thomas, I'm sorry I didn't listen to your advice. I'm sorry I wasn't a good brother to you. Wherever you are, in the forest or heaven or wherever, I love you.

Mom, I'm sorry for not seeing the suffering I caused you, and I'm sorry we couldn't start over again. You thought I was special, a child of God. I betrayed your faith. I love you.

Dad, I'm sorry for lying to you. I love you.

Logan . . . I'm sorry. Logan Albert Canton, I'm just so sorry. I truly am. I did it. I killed you. They can say it was Sanders, but it was me.

All of it was me.

Sanders was right about that much.

I did this.

Nobody else.

The shame, horror, nightmare I've caused—I did it.

I'm so sorry.

They're right above me now.

I've got to get into my tunnel—back into the sewers. But I know they'll find me.

Why can't I stop running?

Why can't I be a man, lay in the bed I've made?

If you're still reading this, then I have only one thing to ask: Take my mistakes, turn them into lessons. My life is over. But you don't have to be like me. You don't have to be a fugitive, a liar, a fuckin' loser.

Goodbye.

> ~ Michael Beatrice Evans

2

Hallow arrived at the Evans' house with Charlie, got out of the car, and headed inside.

"You suppose the forensic team will have anything good for us?"

Charlie scoffed. "What do you think? They didn't find anything in the first couple of days—what makes you think they'll find anything after two weeks?"

"Oh, man . . . ." Hallow stopped in his tracks and looked out the front window.

"What is it?" Charlie turned and looked.

It was Chief Evans and his wife.

They stood there, staring at their house, at the cops, at the chaos.

But they didn't move. It's like they were in shock.

Hallow and Charlie walked outside to meet them.

3

James Evans pulled his police car into his driveway and got out. Abigail followed.

The house was a mess.

There'd been some kind of fire and the entire place was wrapped in yellow crime scene tape.

Hallow and Charlie were walking out the front door towards them.

"Chief." Charlie nodded.

Evans didn't make eye contact. Abigail quietly cried, crossing herself over and over.

Hallow looked down at the floor.

Evans looked over at the house. "Guys, come with me. I think I know where he's been hiding."

He went inside, the two officers following, and went downstairs. In the basement living room, he stopped and pointed at the floor. "Anyone bothered to check the carpets?"

Hallow shook his head. "Everything looked to be in one piece."

Evans pulled the rug away, revealing the bunker's trapdoor. "You might have to blow it off, or cut the lock out. He's probably locked it from the inside."

Hallow rounded up all the officers. "All right, everyone. We think he's in here." He pointed at the bunker door. He looked at Evans. "But he's armed. And if he resists, we'll need to put him down. We clear?"

Everyone nodded.

Evans felt himself nodding, too

4

BANG! BANG! BANG!

"Hey! Open up in there, Michael! You're under arrest!"

Michael stowed his computer and grabbed an AK-47, a Molotov cocktail, a flash grenade, a whole bunch of ammunition, and a Kevlar vest.

"Showtime," he said to himself sadly.

Then a voice stopped him in his tracks. "Michael? It's Dad. Please don't resist arrest. Just come up here so nobody gets hurt."

Michael had an overwhelming desire to surrender.

Dad was calling out to him. But he shook his head and walked over to the tunnel that he had dug.

"I will continue," was all he said as he walked into the tunnel. He didn't even know what he meant.

KABOOM!

Michael spun back, looked at the bunker. The officers had blown off the trapdoor and were dropping down into the bunker. Michael unplugged the flash grenade pin and threw it. There was a burst of light, followed by a series of groans and moans. That would buy him some time.

He fled into the tunnel, made it back into the Normal sewers. He stood for a few seconds, taking in the familiar scenery.

And then he ran.

"Go! Go! Go!" someone shouted. "I can hear him!"

They were catching up.

He ran faster, taking several turns at breakneck speed.

It was no use. So he ran to a corner and crouched, waiting, watching for sudden movements.

Three armed officers charged toward him. Without thinking, he raised his weapon and opened fire. The three officers toppled soundlessly, not like in the movies at all. They just fell. Michael reloaded, turned to see more charging at him. He aimed at each of their feet and fired. Sharp screams rang throughout the tunnels.

BANG!

A gunshot rang out—so loud in the tunnels—and he found himself lying on the sewer floor. He stood up, trying to see the one who'd shot the pipe behind him, back there in the dark. "Come out, coward!" he shouted. "Come out!"

BANG!

Michael screamed and cupped his right ear. "You asshole!" he screeched. "You shot me!"

Officer Hallow shouted back. "This can all end, Michael. Surrender now!"

"I'm not going anywhere!" Michael responded crazily. "You hear me?!" He spotted a dim figure crouching about fifty feet away. He fired. A scream of agony, and a pistol clattered to the floor.

Six more officers carrying assault weapons moved in.

Michael fired again, and men fell.

"Oh, God . . . ." Michael said, staring at their corpses in horror.

He sprinted to the nearest sewer cover, bullets ricocheting, and climbed up. He dug his bottle of Molotov out of his bag, lit it, and threw it into the hole behind him. The sewer erupted in flames, the stench of brimstone rising like a wave. He opened the manhole cover, dragged himself up, and collapsed on the floor.

And then he looked up.

A wooden wall rose up in front of him.

In alarm, he looked back down at the floor. Something was written on the manhole cover.

He read it out loud: "'Satan is beneath you; do not let yourself drown in his temptations.'" He frowned. He felt dizzy.

"Dear God," he whispered.

He'd come out in his mother's church.

"No!" Michael wailed. He ran. Familiar rows of pews filled the floor of a church hall.

It was the very same church in his dreams.

Familiar words echoed in his head.

You must confess, Michael, for you have sinned! You must confess, Michael, for you have sinned! Child of God! Sinner!

"I CONFESS!" Michael screamed. His voice echoed the vaults. "I CONFESS!"

The voices spoke no more.

He stood there for a few seconds, listening to his own heartbeat. He took a few steps toward the front door.

And then a gun pressed against the back of his head and a familiar voice whispered in his ear. "I'm afraid it's over, Michael."

"Sanders." Michael sighed. "Should've known. No bomb can kill you."

"You're right, Michael. Righter than you know."

Michael didn't say anything.

"No pithy comments, boy?" Sanders hissed. "Come

on. You have one more person to kill, Michael. Then your acts will be complete. You've done very well. But there's still more to do—before you die."

Michael clenched his teeth. "I'm not dying today!"

Then he spun and kicked Sanders in the balls.

Before Sanders could react, Michael turned, grabbed his gun, and punched him in the jaw.

Sanders fell back, wobbled, then smiled.

"Good boy," Sanders smiled demonically. "Good boy." His black hair was wild and wiry; a demented fiend. "Send me back to my father, child of God. Do what you're told. Become what I meant for you to become."

Michael pointed the gun at Sanders' head—then pulled the trigger.

BANG!

Sanders fell bonelessly to the floor.

Michael stared at the dead body for a moment, then he dropped his weapon and sprinted out of the church—just running, not looking anywhere. He tripped and fell on the grass. When he stood up, he found himself surrounded by the Normal Police Department.

Hallow was in front, pointing his pistol at him. "You're under arrest, Michael. Anything you say can and will be used against you in a court of law."

Michael nodded, dazed. "I want to call my parents." He reached into his pocket for his phone.

"Keep your hands where I can see them, Michael," Hallow said calmly.

Michael grabbed for his phone.

BANG!

It was like someone had kicked him in the head.

Michael froze in pained shock, an expression of horror locked onto his face.

He reached up, touched the side of his face, and felt blood.

He looked back at Hallow.

"I'm sorry," he said.

He fell to his knees, then collapsed. His heart continued to beat.

In the distance, a siren wailed.

Michael Beatrice Evans had murdered police officers and had executed a man at point-blank range.

Michael had committed his final act of crime.

The Final

1

"Normal officials apprehended suspected terrorist Michael Beatrice Evans two days ago after a shootout in Normal sewers that killed seven police officers and one civilian later identified as David Sanders. A final standoff between the 16-year-old and the police ensued outside an abandoned church. In addition to running a petty fraud ring out of Normal High School, Evans has been charged with the Normal County Depository robbery, several counts of electronic theft, the Normal Bombing, and multiple murders. Evans' hearing is scheduled later this week in the town courthouse."

Michael turned off the TV.

His head ached. It was still wrapped in bandages. He could barely move. His wrist was still handcuffed to the hospital bed.

He shut his eyes.

"I'm sorry," he whispered.

But there was no one there to listen.

2

The trial was held four days later at 8:00 AM. Michael attended in a wheelchair. After several days of testimony and a two-hour recess, the jury unanimously found Michael Beatrice Evans guilty on all counts. Because of his age, he was sentenced to life in prison without parole, rather than the death penalty as sought by the prosecution.

3

The next day, Hallow and Charlie went to the hospital to see Michael. When they arrived, however, he was fast asleep. They stood for a moment, watching the deep rise and fall of the boy's chest. Charlie chewed on a donut. "Look at him," he finally said.

"What?" Hallow asked.

Charlie pointed at the bandages. "There. That's you, man. You did it. You brought him down."

Hallow didn't smile. "I guess. Doesn't make me feel better."

Charlie popped the rest of his donut into his mouth. "What do you mean?"

"Sure, I shot him. But hard to give yourself props when you realize it was just a kid."

Charlie patted him on the shoulder. "Wanna get soe dinner?"

Hallow nodded.

The two officers walked out of the room and closed the door—and the case—behind them.

4

That evening, Michael's parents walked into his room. They carried a birthday cake.

Michael was still sleeping. James frowned. Abigail set the cake on the nightstand.

Then the couple began to sing.

"Happy birthday to you, happy birthday to you, happy birthday, dear Thomas, happy birthday to you."

They blew out the candles.

"This was supposed to be Thomas's birthday, Michael," James said. "He was going to be 18."

"We wanted to celebrate with you," Abigail added. She wiped her eyes.

They ate a slice of cake in silence, but it had no taste.

James looked down on Michael. He took his wife's hand. "We love you, Michael." He cleared his throat. "We always will."

"And we pray for you every day," Abigail said. "God will forgive you, Michael. The Lord's face will shine upon you. Forever and ever. Amen."

They left.

Michael did not wake.

5

Ryan and Kat watched Michael's parents walk down the hall.

When they were gone, Ryan looked at her. "You sure about this?"

"Yeah. Let's go talk to him, even if he can't hear us."

They opened the door and went into the room.

Michael was fast asleep, breathing deeply.

"Hello, Michael," Kat said.

Ryan touched Michael's hand. It was cold. "We just wanted to say that we forgive you, man." He shifted his feet. "I know it seems stupid, but I really hope that—that somewhere, somehow, some part of you can find peace."

"We were there, at the hearing," Kat said. "You just didn't see us. We're sorry. I just . . . I don't know where I'm going with this, but I wanted to tell you that I believe there's a good guy in there somewhere."

6

Much later that night, Thomas walked into Michael's room and closed the door behind him.

"Hello, Michael," Thomas said.

Michael didn't respond.

Thomas was sad that Michael couldn't hear him, that his brother could hear nothing except the sounds of his dreams and thoughts. But he was also relieved, in a way.

"I came to talk. Just talk. It seems cowardly to be here at night, in the dark, when you can't hear me, but . . . . Jesus, I'm not sure I'd be able to talk to you if you *were* awake."

Thomas took a breath and sat down next to the bed.

"First off, it's my birthday. I'm eighteen." He shrugged. "It's fine, I guess. I got a job. I accepted an internship in Los Angeles—."

He stopped and shuddered. "I'm so sorry, Michael. I could've stopped all this. I could've stopped you. I don't know why I didn't . . . . Doesn't matter. I know I failed. I failed our family and our friends. I failed you, Michael. I failed you." Thomas wept at his own words. "I failed you."

He sat there for a while, face in his hands. Then he looked up, stood, and brushed Michael's hair away from his forehead. "Guess you can never be too old for this."

He kissed Michael on the forehead.

"I'll see you in a few years. When we're ready to see each other."

Thomas walked to the door, stopped, and looked back at Michael. "I love you. No matter what. I love you, brother."

And then Thomas turned off the light, leaving his brother to sleep in the darkness.

Acknowledgments

I'd like to thank Peter Schultz, whose unfailing drive and passion helped me through the long, arduous process of book-making. I'd also like to thank the entire team at Silver Goat Media who helped polish the book—seriously, my first draft is unrecognizable from the version you're holding. Enormous thanks also go to my Mom and Dad, my brother Ian, and the rest of my extended family, notably my grandma Marlene; my grandpa George; my cousins Noah, Cody, and Adam; my aunt Jen and uncle Russ; my aunt Shauna and uncle Bob; my godmother Nancy and her family; and my other godmother, Molly. I'd also like to thank Emma Tennyson, who kept me sane through the fall re-write, along with Jonah VanCamp, Trey Johnson, Alex Smith, Lucas Vosburg, Chad Steinke, Ben Walker, Joshua Zosel, Tim Nelson, Philip Johnson, Jack Raaen, Jessica Myxter, Kevin Kennedy, and the organizers of National Novel Writing Month for motivating me to keep going. Finally, I'd like to thank my ninth-grade English teacher, the incredible Jennifer Hoime. Without her constant faith in me, without her push to get me writing in the fall of 2015, *The Seven Acts* wouldn't exist. From the bottom of my heart, thank you.

About the Author

Malcolm Strand graduated from Fargo South High School in the spring of 2019. He'll be attending Drake University in the fall of 2019, where he'll pursue studies in Political Science. Malcolm has been writing since he was five years old, his first effort being a children's book titled *Ripped Pants*. Upon encouragement from his freshman English teacher, Mrs. Hoime, Malcolm began work on a project during National Novel Writing Month in November of 2015, a project that would eventually become *The Seven Acts*—this book!

www.ingramcontent.com/pod-product-compliance
Lightning Source LLC
Chambersburg PA
CBHW020552020726
47494CB00006B/2044